INTO THIN AIR

MARY ELLEN PORTER

 HARLEQUIN® LOVE INSPIRED® SUSPENSE

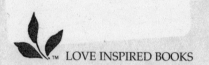

LOVE INSPIRED BOOKS

Recycling programs
for this product may
not exist in your area.

ISBN-13: 978-0-373-44671-1

Into Thin Air

www.Harlequin.com

Printed in U.S.A.

Many are the plans in a man's heart,
but it is the Lord's purpose that prevails.
–Proverbs 19:21

To Eldridge, for always believing in me,
even when I doubted myself. Your love, support and unfailing
encouragement are the foundation of all my achievements.

To my children, Skylar and Trey.
No mother could be more proud than I am of you;
you make me smile every day. May you find God's special
purpose for your lives within your hopes and dreams.

And to my sister, Shirlee McCoy, whose ten years of
persistent and "gentle" prodding resulted in this book.
Smart. Talented. Tenacious. Stubborn. A definite combination
for success. It's finally my turn to say "Me, too." Thank you
for never letting me forget my dreams. This one's for you.

ONE

It was a passing glimpse, no more. A young teen walking slowly along the edge of the darkening side street, a violin case tucked in the crook of her arm, her face illuminated by her cell phone screen as she furiously texted, aware of nothing but the phone in her hand.

The van made even less of an impression, the driver all but invisible as the vehicle passed Laney Kensington's Jeep Wrangler.

Both should have been easy to ignore, but they nagged at Laney's mind—made the hair on the back of her neck prickle. Laney told herself it was just her imagination getting the best of her—but she couldn't simply drive on.

Call it intuition, call it divine intervention—Laney called it never wrong.

She'd never ignored it on a search. She wouldn't ignore it now.

She glanced in the rearview mirror, pulse jumping as the van swung a wide U-turn and headed back toward the girl. Laney did the same, stepping on the gas, her Jeep surging forward.

The slowing van closed in on the girl. She finally looked up, eyes widening as a figure jumped out and sprinted toward her. The violin dropped from her arms and she tried to run.

Too little, too late.

The man was on her in a flash, hand over her mouth, dragging her toward the van. In seconds they'd be gone. One more child missing. One more family broken.

Not today. Not if Laney could help it.

Although it had been years since she'd last prayed, Laney found herself whispering a silent plea to God, begging Him for help that deep down she knew would never come. She'd learned a long time ago that the only one she could depend on was herself.

Putting her trust anywhere else was just too risky.

The van was right in front of her, and there was only one thing Laney could think to do to stop the kidnapping. She braced for impact, ramming the front of the van with her Jeep in the hope of disabling it. In the back seat, Murphy yelped at the jarring stop; there was no time to comfort the dog.

Leaping from the Jeep, Laney threw herself at the would-be kidnapper. His weight off-balance from the struggling child, he tumbled over. The girl went with him, her high-pitched scream piercing the still air. Laney snagged the girl's hand, yanking her to her feet.

"Run!" she shouted, but the kidnapper was on his feet again, snatching a handful of the girl's shirt and dragging her back.

"Back off!" he commanded, his voice chilling.

Laney slammed into him again, this time with so much force they all fell in a tangled mass of limbs, pushing and grabbing and struggling. The kidnapper grunted as Laney kneed him in the kidney. His grip on the girl loosened, and Laney shoved her from the heap.

But the kidnapper would not let his prey go without a fight. He reverse punched Laney, propelling her backward. She tumbled onto damp grass, her head slamming into hard earth. She had a moment of panic as blackness edged in. She could *not* lose consciousness. She willed herself up, lunging toward the struggling pair as they neared the van. Laney yanked the guy's arm and slammed her foot into the back of his knee. He cursed, swinging around, the girl between them.

"I said *back off*!" he growled, his dark eyes filled with fury, his hand clamped firmly over the girl's mouth.

Laney eased around so that she stood between him and the van. She saw that the girl was still fighting against his hold, but her efforts were futile. She met Laney's eyes, the fear in her gaze something Laney knew she would never forget.

It's okay, Laney wanted to say. *He's not going to take you. I won't let him.*

"Let her go," Laney demanded.

"I don't think so." The man glanced just beyond Laney's shoulder, a cold smile curving his lips.

The girl stilled, her eyes widening.

Laney knew without even looking that someone was behind her.

Her blood ran cold, but she turned, ready to fight as many people as it took for as long as she had to. Eventually, another car would come, someone would call the police, help would arrive. She just had to hold the kidnappers off long enough for that to happen.

A shadowy figured jumped from the van's open door. Laney had the impression of height and weight, of dark hair and cold eyes, but it was the gun that caught and held her attention. Although the gunman was shorter and more wiry than his stocky partner, the firearm in his hand made him far more lethal.

"Don't move," he snapped, the gun pointed straight at Laney's heart.

Laney stopped in her tracks, hands in the air in a display of unarmed surrender.

She wanted him to think she'd given up; she needed him off guard. She had to get the gun out of his hands, and she had to free the girl.

"Get the kid in the van before someone else comes by," the gunman ordered his accomplice.

"What do we do with the woman?" the other man asked as he dragged the child around Laney, grunting and tightening his grip as the girl's sneaker-clad foot caught his shin.

"Get rid of her. She's a loose end. No witnesses, remember?" The words were spoken with cold malice that sent a wave of fear up Laney's spine.

No cars coming, nothing to hide behind. No matter what direction Laney ran, a bullet could easily find her. If the girl was going to survive, if *Laney* was going to, the gunman had to be taken down. Laney braced herself for action, waiting for an opening that she was afraid wouldn't come.

Please, she prayed silently. *Just give me a chance.*

The girl grunted, trying to scream against the hand pressed to her face. They were close to the van door, so close that Laney knew it was just a matter of seconds before the girl was shoved in.

"Bite him!" she yelled.

"Shut up!" the gunman barked, glancing over his shoulder to check on his accomplice's progress. That was the opening Laney needed. She threw herself at his gun hand. He cursed, the gun dropping to the ground. They both reached for it, Laney's fingers brushing cold metal, victory right beneath her palm. He slammed his fist into her jaw and she flew back, her grip on the gun lost in a wave of shocking pain. A dog growled, the harsh sound mixing with the frantic rush of Laney's pulse.

Murphy! She'd not given him the release command, yet he raced toward them, teeth bared.

The man raised the gun. Laney tried to scramble out of

the way as he pulled the trigger. Hot pain seared through her temple, and she fell, Murphy's well-muscled body the last thing she saw as she sank into darkness.

Grayson DeMarco rushed through Anne Arundel Medical Center's fluorescently lit hallway, scanning the staff and visitors moving through the corridor. He'd been working this case for almost a year. He'd dogged every lead to every dead end, traveling from California to Boston and down to Baltimore, and he'd always been a few steps behind, a few days too late.

Sixteen children abducted. Four states. Not one single break.

Until tonight.

Finally the abductors had made a mistake.

A young girl was missing. The police had received her parents' frantic call less than thirty minutes after a woman had been found shot and unconscious on the sidewalk, a violin case and cell phone lying on the grass near her. The case had the missing girl's name on it.

Grayson had been called immediately, state PD moving quickly. They felt the pressure, too; they could see the tally of the area's missing children going up.

Like Grayson, they could hear the clock ticking.

They'd found a gun at the scene, spattered with blood, lying in the small island of grass that separated the sidewalk from the street. Grayson hoped it would yield useable prints and a DNA profile that could possibly lead him one step closer to the answers he was searching for.

He prayed it would, but he wasn't counting on it.

He'd been to the scene. He'd peered into an abandoned Jeep, lights still on, driver's door open. He'd opened the victim's wallet, seen her identification—Laney Kensington, five feet three inches and one hundred ten pounds. He'd gotten a good look at the German shepherd that might have been responsible for stopping the kidnappers before they were able to kill the woman. He'd pieced together an idea of what might have happened, but he needed to talk to Laney Kensington, find out what had really gone down, how much she'd seen. More importantly, he needed to know exactly how valuable that information might be to the case he was working.

Time was of the essence if Grayson had any chance of bringing these children home.

Failure was not an option.

A police officer stood guard outside the woman's room, his arms crossed over his chest, his expression neutral. He didn't move as Grayson approached, didn't acknowledge him at all until Grayson flashed his badge. "Special Agent Grayson DeMarco, FBI."

"Detective Paul Jensen, Maryland State Police," the detective responded. "No one's allowed in to see the victim. If that's why you're here, you may as well turn around and—"

He cut the man off. "We don't have time to play jurisdiction games, Detective. As of tonight, three kids are missing from Maryland in just under six weeks."

"I'm well aware of that, but I have my orders, and until I hear from my supervisor that you're approved to go in there, you're out."

"How about you give him a call, then?" Grayson reached past the detective and opened the door, ignoring the guy's angry protest as he walked into the cool hospital room.

The witness lay unconscious under a mound of sheets and blankets, her dark auburn hair tangled around a face that was pale and still streaked with dried blood. Faint signs of bruising shadowed her jaw, made more evident by the harsh hospital lights. A bandage covered her temple, and an IV line snaked out from beneath the sheets. She appeared delicate, almost fragile, not at all what he was expecting given her part in the events of the night. Fortunately, as fragile as she appeared, the bullet had merely grazed her temple and she would eventually make a full recovery.

Unfortunately, Grayson didn't have the luxury of waiting for her to heal. He needed to speak to her. The sooner the better.

He moved toward the bed, trying to ignore the pine scent of floor cleaner, the harsh overhead lights, the IV line. They reminded him of things he was better off forgetting, of a time when he hadn't been sure he could keep doing what he did.

He pulled a chair to the side of the bed and sat, glancing at Detective Jensen, who'd followed him into the room. "Aren't you supposed to be guarding the door?"

"I'm guarding the witness, and I could force you out of here," the detective retorted, his eyes flashing with irritation and a hint of worry.

"What would be the point? You know I've got jurisdiction."

The detective offered no response. Grayson hadn't expected him to. Policies and protocol didn't bring abducted kids back to their parents, and wasting time fighting over jurisdiction wasn't going to accomplish anything.

"Look," he said, meeting the detective's dark eyes. "I'm not here to step on toes. I'm here to find these kids. There's still a chance we can bring them home. All of them. How about you keep that in mind?"

The guy muttered something under his breath and stalked out of the room.

That was fine with Grayson. He preferred to be alone with the witness when she woke. He wanted every bit of information she had, every minute detail. He didn't want it second- or third-hand, didn't want to get it after it had already been said a few times. He needed her memories fresh and clear, undiluted by time or speculation.

Laney groaned softly and began to stir. Just for a moment, Grayson felt like a voyeur. It seemed almost wrong to be sitting over her bed waiting for her to gain consciousness. She needed family or friends around her. Not a jaded FBI agent with his own agenda.

He leaned in toward Laney. Though only moments ago she had appeared to be on the verge of waking, she had grown still again.

"Laney?" he said softly. "Can you hear me?"

He leaned in closer. "Laney?"

She stirred, eyes moving rapidly behind closed lids. Was she caught in a dream, or a memory? he wondered.

"Wake up, Laney." He reached out, resting his hand gently on her forearm.

She came up swinging, her fist grazing his chin, her eyes wild. She swung again, and Grayson did the only thing he could. He ducked.

TWO

"Calm down," a man said, his warm fingers curved around Laney's wrist. She tried to pull away but couldn't quite find the strength. Her head throbbed, the pungent smell of antiseptic filled her nose, and she couldn't manage to do more than stare into the stranger's dark-lashed blue eyes.

Not the kidnapper's eyes. Not the eyes of his accomplice. She wasn't lying on the pavement in the dark. There was no Jeep. No van. No struggling young girl with terror in her eyes. Nothing but cream-colored walls and white sheets and a man who could have been anyone looking at her expectantly.

"What happened? How did I get here?" she asked, levering up on her elbows, the hospital room too bright, her heart beating an erratic cadence in her chest.

"A couple of joggers found you lying on the sidewalk," the man responded. "Do you remember anything about tonight?"

Anything?

She remembered *everything*—heading home from Murphy's training session, seeing the girl and the van, struggling and fighting and failing. Again.

"Yes," she mumbled, willing away nausea and the deep pain of failure.

"Good." He smiled, his expression changing from harsh and implacable to something that looked like triumph. "That's going to help a lot."

"Help who?" Because her actions tonight certainly hadn't helped the girl or her family. Overwhelming sadness welled up within her, but Laney forced it back. She had to get a grip on herself. She had no idea how long she'd been unconscious, what had happened to Murphy, or most importantly, if the police even knew a child had been taken.

"I'm Special Agent Grayson DeMarco with the FBI," the man explained. "I'm hoping you can help with a case I'm working on."

"I'm not worried about your case, Agent DeMarco. I'm worried about the girl who was kidnapped tonight." She shoved the sheets off her legs and sat up. Her head swam, the pain behind her eyes nearly blinding her, but she had to get to a phone. She needed to tell Police Chief Kent Andrews what had happened. They needed to start searching immediately if there was any chance to save the child. And there *had* to be a chance.

"The girl *is* my case—and several other children like her," Agent DeMarco responded. "The local police are at the scene of the kidnapping. They're gathering evidence and doing everything they can to locate her, but she's not the only victim. If you've been watching the local news, you know that."

Because he seemed to expect a response, Laney nodded, realizing immediately that was a mistake as pain exploded through her temple. Her stomach churned.

"Lie down." Somehow Agent DeMarco was standing, his hands on her shoulders as he urged her back onto the pillows. "You're not going to do anyone any good if you're unconscious again." The words were harsh, but his touch was light.

Laney eyed him critically. She'd been working around

law enforcement—local as well as Secret Service and DEA—for much of her adult life. She knew how the agencies operated. The FBI wouldn't be called in on an isolated, random child abduction.

"I'm fine," she muttered, pushing the button on the bed railing until the mattress raised her to a sitting position.

"You came within an inch of dying, Laney. I wouldn't call that fine." He settled back into the chair, his black tactical pants, T-shirt and jacket making him look more like a mercenary than an officer of the law.

She gingerly fingered a thick bandage that covered her temple and knew Agent DeMarco was right. "Murphy must have thrown his aim off."

"Murphy is the dog that was found at the scene?"

"Yes, I need to—"

"The local police have him. I was told he was being brought back to the kennel."

"Told by whom?" she asked. Agent DeMarco was saying all the right things, but she didn't know him, hadn't seen any identification, still wasn't a hundred percent convinced he was who he said he was.

"Chief Kent Andrews. He'll probably be here shortly. He's still overseeing the scene."

"I'd like to speak with him." She and Kent went back a couple of years. She often worked with the Maryland State Police K-9 team, correcting training issues with both the dogs and their handlers in an unofficial capacity.

"You will, but I need to ask you a few questions first."

"How about you show me some ID? Then you can ask your questions."

The request didn't surprise Grayson. He'd been told that Laney knew her way around law enforcement and that she wasn't someone who'd blindly follow orders. While working with the state K-9 team as a dog trainer, her skills with

animals and the trainees alike had garnered the respect
of the police chief and his men. More than that, Grayson got the distinct impression that Kent Andrews really
liked Laney as a person and wasn't surprised at all that
she would put herself in danger to help another.

"Sure." Grayson fished his ID out of his pocket, handed
it to her.

She studied it, her wavy hair sliding across her cheeks
and hiding her expression. She didn't trust him. That much
was obvious, but she finally handed the ID back. "What
do you want to know?" she asked.

"Everything," he responded, taking a small notepad and
pen from his jacket pocket. "All the details of what happened tonight. What you saw. Who you saw. Don't leave
anything out. Even the smallest detail could be important."

"I was on my way back from Davidsonville Park with
Murphy when I saw her."

"Was she alone?"

"Yes. She was walking by herself. I always hate seeing that. I can't even count the number of kids my team
and I have searched for who were out by themselves when
they disappeared." She pinched the bridge of her nose and
frowned. "Sorry, I'm getting off track. This headache…"
She shook her head slightly and winced.

"Want me to call the nurse and get you something for
the pain?" He would, but he didn't want to. He needed her
as clear-headed as she could be.

She must have sensed that. She rested her head on the
pillow. "That would be nice, but I'm not sure I'll be any
good to anyone filled with a bunch of painkillers."

"Don't suffer for your cause, Laney. If you need pain
medication, take it."

She smiled at that, a real smile that brightened her
eyes and somehow made the smattering of freckles on
her cheeks and nose more noticeable. She was pretty in a

girl-next-door kind of way. He tried to imagine her taking on a guy with a gun. Couldn't quite do it. "I hate taking narcotics," she muttered. "I'll ask for Tylenol later."

He wasn't going to argue with her. "You saw the girl walking alone," he prompted her.

"Yes. I was headed home. A van was coming toward me in the opposite direction. We passed the girl at nearly the same time."

"Passed her?" He'd assumed she'd driven up as the girl was being abducted.

"Yes. The van made me think of the news reports of other abductions in the area. I glanced in the rearview mirror and saw the van U-turn. I did the same." Laney looked away as if unable to meet his gaze. "Unfortunately, it reached her first. She was texting and didn't even see them coming."

"Could you see the color of the van?"

"Not initially, but I got a good look at it when I rammed it with my jeep. It was a dark charcoal gray. My front fender probably scraped off some of the paint. It will have a fresh dent on the front passenger side…" Laney's voice faltered.

"Did you see the person who grabbed her? Can you describe him?" he asked, every cell in his body waiting for the answer. If she saw the guy, if she had a description, if there was DNA on the gun, they'd finally have something to go on.

"I had a pretty clear view. There were streetlights and the headlights from my Jeep."

"Tell me what you remember. Don't hold anything back." Grayson urged.

"He was about six-foot-one with the build of an ex–football player—beefy but not in great shape anymore. His hair was dark brown and cropped close, like a military cut. He was wearing jeans with a black hooded sweatshirt and black work boots. He had brown eyes and an olive complexion. I saw part of a tattoo on the back of his neck, sticking out from the collar of his sweatshirt, but I didn't get a good look at it." She paused, frowned. "He wasn't alone. There was another guy in the van. He came out to help. He was shorter—I'd guess about five-foot-ten. Thin—like a runner's build. His hair was light brown, nose slightly crooked. He was the one with the gun."

Grayson scribbled notes furiously. "What about their ages?"

"Early to mid-thirties. Both of them."

"Did either speak?"

"Both did, but they didn't call each other by name."

Too bad. That would have been another lead to follow. "What about accents?"

"None that I could distinguish."

"Did the girl seem to know her kidnappers?"

"If she knew them, it didn't show. As far as I could tell, she was an arbitrary target, but the way the van was parked would have made it nearly impossible for anyone on the street to see the kidnappers. It seemed random…but not."

"How so?"

"Like they were trolling the streets looking for someone, but once they picked a target their actions were deliberate—no hesitation—like they'd done the same thing before. If I hadn't been there, the girl—"

"Olivia Henley. She's thirteen. She was on her way home from her weekly music lesson. Her parents reported her missing shortly after the joggers found you." He wanted Laney to have a name to go with the face. He wanted her to know that there was a family who was missing a child. Not because he wanted her to feel guilty or obligated, but because he wanted her to understand how serious things were, how imperative it was that she cooperate.

"Olivia," she repeated quietly. "If I hadn't been there,

she would have disappeared, and no one would have known what happened." She paused, her face so pale, he thought she might lose consciousness again. "If only I had done something differently, maybe she wouldn't have been taken."

"You did what you could, which is more than most would."

"But it wasn't enough, was it?" She leveled her gaze at him, surprising him with the depth of anger he saw reflected in her eyes. "That little girl is gone, Agent De-Marco. Her bed will be empty tonight."

Grayson recognized and understood her frustration. So many children went missing every day, and not all of them would make it home. He knew that better than most. "Not because of you, Laney. Because of the kidnappers."

"That's no consolation to her parents." Laney closed her eyes. "I wish I could have saved her."

"You still might be able to. If you're up to it, I'd like you to meet with a sketch arti—"

"I'm up to it. Let's go." Before the words were out of her mouth, she was up from bed, the white cotton sheet draped around her shoulders like a cape as she wobbled toward the door, the IV pole trailing along behind her.

"I didn't mean now," he said, taking three long strides to beat her to the door and slapping his palm against it so that she couldn't open it. "And I didn't mean you should walk out of here with an IV line attached to your arm, either."

"Then bring the sketch artist here." She turned to face him, swaying a little in the process. "The sooner you have an image of these guys, the sooner everyone can be on the lookout for them. If you really think Olivia can be saved, there's no time to lose."

She was right, of course. About all of it. There was only one problem with her plan, and it was a big one.

"We're not bringing the sketch artist here," he said,

leading her back toward the bed. "You'd better lie down before you fall down."

She dropped into the chair instead, her face ashen, her eyes a dark emerald green against the pallor. "Why *not* bring the sketch artist here?" Her voice had lost some of its strength, but she hadn't lost any of her determination. "We're wasting time talking when we could be—"

"As far as the kidnappers know, you're dead, Laney," he said, cutting her off.

"What?"

"Dead. Deceased. Gone."

She rolled her eyes. "I know what you meant, Agent. I want to know *why* they think I'm dead."

"You were shot. Murphy might have distracted the shooter, but you went down. You were bleeding enough to make anyone think you'd been mortally wounded. The joggers who found you were a couple of teenage girls. They panicked, called 911 and reported a body. No one knows who you are or that you survived except the first responders and the hospital staff treating you, and they've been asked to keep it quiet. As far as the media and the public are concerned, Jane Doe was shot and killed on Ashley Street at approximately seven-thirty this evening. I'd like to keep your identity quiet for as long as possible."

Laney frowned. "Protecting my identity is the last thing we need to worry about."

"I disagree."

"Maybe you should explain why."

Grayson hesitated. Andrews had assured him that Laney was as good as they came, loyal and trustworthy. Even so, Grayson was reluctant to divulge too much. He was used to working alone. Putting his trust in God and his own abilities above all else. He had this one perfect lead, and he didn't want anything to keep it from panning out. "For now, I need you to trust that I'm making the best decisions I can for you and Olivia."

"For now," Laney agreed, struggling to her feet. "But you need to know that I'm not going to spend much time sitting around this hospital room while you make decisions for me. That's not the way I work."

She jabbed the call button on the bed railing, and he had visions of her walking out of the hospital in the mint-green hospital gown, the bandage on her forehead a glaring testimony to her injury. If the kidnappers were hanging around hoping to hear rumors confirming Jane Doe's death, they might catch a glimpse of Laney and follow her home. That was the last thing Grayson wanted.

He was all too aware that his biggest hope just might lie on the slender shoulders of Laney Kensington. If she could identify the kidnappers, he would be one step closer to saving Olivia—and the other children. He needed her help. And to get it, he had to give her some measure of trust.

"Then tell me how you *do* work," he offered. "And, let's see what kind of a compromise we can reach."

"I'm not looking for compromise. I need to know what's going on. Let's start with what you've got on these kidnappings."

It went against his nature to give her the information. He'd been keeping everything close to the vest. The less media coverage about the kidnappings, the better, as far as he was concerned. He was closing in on the perps. He could feel it, and he didn't want to risk scaring them off. He needed them to feel comfortable and confident. Their cockiness would be key to bringing them down.

On the other hand, he couldn't risk having Laney go maverick on him. If what the police chief had said about her was true, she knew enough about search and rescue and about police work to be dangerous. He had no doubt that she understood she could walk out of the hospital and away from him altogether. He had nothing on her and no legal means to keep her where she was. And if the kidnappers caught even a glimpse of her, the damage would be done. She'd gotten a good look at the kidnappers. He could only assume they'd gotten a good look at her, too. Once they knew she was alive, how quickly could they find her if they put their minds to it?

"Okay," he finally said. "Just have a seat and I'll tell you as much as I can."

She hesitated, her face drawn. Finally she complied, dropping back into the chair and fixing all of her attention on him.

"Well?" she prodded.

He pulled a chair over and sat.

They were knee to knee, the fabric of his pants brushing against the sheet she'd wrapped herself in, the IV pole just to the side of her chair. She looked young and vulnerable, her life way too easy to snuff out. That thought brought memories of another time, and for a moment, Grayson was in different hospital room, looking into another pale face. He hadn't been able to save Andrea, but he was going to do everything in his power to make sure Laney survived.

THREE

"What I am about to tell you is sensitive," Agent De-Marco said. "I need your word that you'll keep it confidential."

"Of course," Laney agreed.

"Good, because you're the only witness to a kidnapping that is connected to the abduction of two other children over the past six weeks."

"That's not a secret, Agent. It's been in the news for a few weeks." In fact, those abductions—one outside of DC and the other in Annapolis—had been nagging at her when she saw the van on Ashley Street.

"There have also been similar clusters of child abductions in two other states."

She definitely *hadn't* heard that before. "How many children are we talking about?"

"Thirteen others, so far. Not including the three from this area."

"Sixteen kids missing? I'd think that would be all over the news."

"It has been. Regional news only. The first seven disappeared from the Los Angeles area over a four-month period. The next six disappeared from the Boston vicinity in just under three months. In many cases, there were reports of a dark van in the area around the time of the abductions."

"Just like the van tonight."

He nodded. "Your description is the most detailed, but other witnesses mentioned a dark panel van. Unfortunately, no one has seen the driver. You're the first witness we have who's seen everything—the van, the missing child, the kidnappers. It's the break I've been waiting for, and I don't want anything to jeopardize it. We need to keep the fact that you survived quiet for as long as possible. The less the kidnappers realize we know, the easier it will be to close in on them."

"I understand. I won't tell anyone."

"It's not as simple as that. The kidnappers are aware that you were shot. They could have followed the ambulance to the hospital. They could be waiting around, hoping to hear some information that will confirm your death or refute it."

"Why would they bother? I saw them, but I don't know who they are."

"You've worked with law enforcement for years, Laney. You understand how this works. They tried to silence you to keep you from reporting what you witnessed. If they see that they failed, they may try again."

"But is sticking around to kill me really worth the risk when they could just skip town with the kids and disappear?" That's what she thought they'd do, but she wasn't sure how clear her thinking was. Her head ached so badly, she just wanted to close her eyes.

"This trafficking ring is extensive," Agent DeMarco explained. "We've had reports that the children are being transported overseas and sold into slavery. This is a multitier operation that isn't just being run here in the United States. There are kids missing in Europe, in Canada, in Asia, and each time, the kidnappings occur in clusters.

Five, six, seven kids from a region go missing, and then nothing."

"Except families left with broken hearts and no answers," Laney murmured, the thought of all those kids, all those parents and siblings, all those empty bedrooms and empty hearts making her heart ache and head pound even more.

"Right." Agent DeMarco leaned forward, and Laney could see the black rim around his blue irises, the dark stubble on his chin. He had a tiny scar at the corner of his left brow and a larger one close to his hairline. He looked tough and determined, and for some reason she found that reassuring.

"Olivia's abduction makes the third in this area," Agent DeMarco continued, "but if their pattern holds, they plan to target more from the surrounding area before moving the kids."

"It seems a safer bet for them to cut their losses and move on," she said doubtfully.

"We're talking money, Laney. A lot of it. Money is a great motivator. It can turn ordinary men into extraordinary criminals."

"And kidnappers into murderers?"

"That, too." He stood and paced across the room. "This is a business for them, with schedules to keep and deliveries to make. I'm certain the children are being held somewhere while they wait for prearranged transport out of the country. Moving them to another location would also risk exposure. You were shot tonight because they can't afford any witnesses. They need to buy time to get their quota of children ready for delivery. With you dead or incapacitated, the immediate threat of exposure is gone."

"So as long as they believe I died, it's business as usual."

Agent DeMarco nodded, returning to his chair, and leveling his gaze on her. "The longer it takes for the kidnappers to realize you survived, the better it will be for everyone."

"Not for Olivia," she pointed out, that image—the one of the girl, her eyes wide, begging for help—filling her mind again. She'd failed to save her, and that knowledge was worse than the pain in her head, worse than the nausea. "She's terrified and alone. She doesn't care who knows what. All she cares about is getting home."

"You're wrong. It does matter for Olivia," Agent De-Marco responded. "There's a chance that we can reunite Olivia with her family, but only if the kidnappers aren't scared into moving early. All we have to do is find Olivia's kidnappers, and we'll find her. We'll find them all."

His words made her heart jump, and she was almost ready to spring up from the chair and start looking in every place they could possibly be. "Then why are we sitting here? Why aren't we out searching for them?"

"Chief Andrews said you'd ask that," he responded, a half smile curving his lips. "He told me to assure you that he has a K-9 team working the scene."

But Laney knew they'd not find much. Olivia had been driven off in a van. Even her retired search dog, Jax, who had been one of the best air scent dogs in the country, wouldn't be able to pick up her scent under those circumstances.

She recognized that, but still, she wanted to be in on the action in a way she hadn't wanted to be since the accident that took her teammates' lives. The accident that had prompted her to leave her search-and-rescue work behind and put Jax into early retirement. The thought stole some of her energy, and she sank back against the chair. "That's good. If there's something to find, they'll uncover it."

"That's what I've been told. You've been working with them for a while?"

She had. For nearly two years now. She volunteered her

time to ensure high-drive, problem dogs were given the chance to succeed. She'd helped train several dogs that had been like Murphy—problematic but with obvious promise. Although Kent made repeated offers to make her role with the department more permanent, she was reluctant to fall back into the stressful life of a contract employee. Besides, her own clients kept her busy enough. "Unofficially. I own a private boarding and training facility in Davidsonville. Murphy is the most recent in a line of MPD K-9s I've worked with."

"Murphy." His smile broadened. "He's quite a dog."

"He's quite a problem child, but we're working on it."

"He came through for you tonight," he pointed out.

"Yes. Though technically, he's supposed to leave the vehicle only on command."

"Well, in this case, it's a good thing he didn't."

"I think seeing the gun set him off. We just started working with firearms last week, and he's making good progress." Better than she had hoped. She was pleased at how quickly Murphy was improving after being booted out of the MPD K-9 program once. He was a little high-energy and distractible, but he possessed the important shepherd traits—intelligence and loyalty.

Agent DeMarco smiled. "Andrews and the K-9 handlers certainly seemed happy the dog came through for you."

She forced herself out of the chair, every muscle in her body protesting. "Speaking of which, I need to talk to Kent. I don't suppose you have my things?"

"Purse? Cell Phone? House keys?"

"Yes."

"They've been collected as evidence. Your Jeep was impounded, too. And your clothes—" his gaze dropped from her face to the cotton hospital gown "—were also taken as evidence."

"I guess I'll be flagging a taxi in this hospital gown,"

she responded. She wasn't going to stay in the hospital any longer than necessary. Her business was thriving. That meant plenty of work to do at the kennel. She was hoping that would keep her mind off her failures. She didn't need to spend months mourning what she hadn't been able to do for Olivia. She'd been down that path before, and it hadn't led to anything but misery.

"Leaving in a hospital gown isn't going to work. It's a surefire way to get the wrong people's attention. When you leave, we're going to do everything possible to make sure no one notices you."

"That's going to be really difficult with—"

There was a sudden commotion outside the door, a flurry of movement and voices that had Agent DeMarco pivoting toward the sound.

"Stay there," he commanded, striding toward the door and yanking it open.

His broad back blocked Laney's view, and she moved closer, trying to see over his shoulder. A police officer stood in the doorway, back to the room.

"Ma'am, I told you no one can enter without permission," he said to someone Laney couldn't see.

"Ridiculous," a woman responded, the voice as familiar as the morning sun.

Great-Aunt Rose. Someone must have called her.

"Aunt Rose, don't—" Laney began.

Too late. Rose somehow darted through the blockade of masculinity, slipping past the officer.

Agent DeMarco stepped to the side, letting her by. Obviously he wasn't worried about a five-foot-nothing octogenarian. The officer, on the other hand, looked quite disgruntled.

"Do you want me to cuff you, ma'am?" he shouted.

"Don't be silly, boy. I'm too old. You'd break my brittle wrists." Rose smoothed loose strands of silver hair back into her neat bun, then brushed invisible lint from her beige slacks. Her gaze settled on Agent DeMarco for a moment before her focus shifted to Laney.

"You're awake! Thank the good Lord for His mercy!" she cried, hefting an oversize bag onto the bed.

"Yeah," the officer sputtered. "She's awake, and I'm going to lose my job."

"Now, why would you go and do something like that?" Aunt Rose asked, completely unfazed by the commotion she'd caused. Typical Rose. Always in the midst of trouble and never quite sure why.

"My aunt is notorious for getting what she wants," Laney cut in. "I'm sure Chief Andrews will understand the position you were in."

"He might, but I don't," the officer responded irritably. "But I guess as long as she's your aunt, I'll go back to my post."

He returned to the corridor, closing the door with a little more force than necessary.

"You've annoyed him, Aunt Rose," Laney said.

"And you've annoyed me. Getting yourself shot up and tossed into the hospital and interrupting a perfectly wonderful book club meeting," Rose responded. She touched Laney's cheek and shook her head. "What in the world happened? I mean, Tommy said you'd been shot...but I figured he's so old, he probably got it wrong."

"Tom is barely sixty, Aunt Rose, and you know it." Laney sighed. Her aunt and the deputy chief of police Tom Wallace had never hit it off. She'd have to remember to thank him for calling Rose. The poor guy tried to avoid Rose as often as possible.

"But he acts like he's a hundred, 'bout as fun as a stick in the mud. Remember that picnic at the kennel last year? He—"

"Aunt Rose, please. I'm not in the mood for trips down

memory lane," Laney said, her head pounding with re-
newed vigor.

"Are you in the mood to sit down?" Agent DeMarco
asked, taking Laney's arm and urging her to the chair she'd
abandoned. "You look like you probably should."

She settled into the chair, watching with horror as Rose
peered up at Agent DeMarco. If Laney's brain had been
functioning at full capacity, she'd have found a way to refocus her aunt's attention. As it was, all she could do was
hope that Rose didn't say anything she'd regret. Or, more
to the point, that *Laney* would regret.

"You must be that FBI agent Tommy told me about,"
Rose said with a smile.

"Yes, ma'am. Special Agent Grayson DeMarco."

"Well, I'm too old to be remembering all those names
and titles—what's your mama call you?"

Agent DeMarco smiled at that. "She calls me Gray."

"Well, then, Gray it is, and you can call me Rose. None
of those niceties like 'ma'am'…that just makes me feel old."
Rose plopped down in the chair Agent DeMarco had va-
cated only moments ago.

"How'd you get here Aunt Rose? I hope you didn't
drive," Laney said. The thought of Rose speeding down
Route 50 was not especially comforting.

"Of course not. You know my license was temporarily
revoked after that unfortunate incident at Davis's Plant
Emporium. Really, I don't understand why everyone was
so upset—it was only a couple of bushes and some potted
plants, after all…but that's neither here nor there." Rose
shook her head and patting Laney's knee. "Tommy drove
me. Kent sent him to pick me up. I imagine Tommy will
be along soon." She lowered her voice to a decidedly loud
whisper. "I made him drop me off at the door so no one
would see us walk in together—that's how rumors get

started. Before you know it, the whole congregation will be saying I was arrested or some such nonsense."

"Rose," Agent DeMarco said, "did Deputy Chief Wallace explain that we need to keep the details of this situation quiet?"

"Yes, yes. He explained. No need to worry about me. My mind is a steel trap, and my lips are sealed." Rose put a hand up as if waving away the agent's concerns, then turned to Laney. "So, how on earth did you get yourself shot?"

Was Laney allowed to mention the kidnapping? She didn't know, so she kept it brief. "I witnessed a crime and tried to intervene."

"I bet you weren't carrying that mace I gave you last Christmas, were you?" Rose frowned. "That stuff's supposed to be powerful enough to stop a bear in its tracks. A criminal would probably have a hard time aiming at you with that in his eyes. I've got my can of it right in that bag. Anyone tries to come at us, I'll take him down."

Grayson would almost have liked to see that.

Laney's aunt looked about as old as Methuselah, but she moved like a woman much younger. He could picture her reaching into the bag, yanking out the spray and taking down a kidnapper.

A quick rap at the door and a young female doctor walked in, followed closely by Deputy Chief Tom Wallace. Grayson had met him at the crime scene, and he'd liked the guy immediately. Though old-school and by-the-book, he didn't have any compunction about sharing information with the FBI.

"Agent DeMarco," Wallace said, "the chief said to let you know they've finished with the crime scene. He's going to the precinct to make sure the blood and finger prints on the gun are expedited for processing."

"Thanks, Deputy." So far he liked the way Chief Andrews handled things, and he wasn't surprised that Andrews was taking a very personal interest in the case. "I may head that way myself after Laney is discharged."

"*If* she's discharged," Wallace replied. "The *doctor* will decide that and *then* we can come up with a plan for getting her out of here."

They weren't going to do anything. Grayson had a plan, and he was sticking to it. He didn't bother telling Wallace that. The doctor was already leaning over Laney, flashing a light in her eyes, asking about pain level, nausea, dizziness. Laney answered quietly.

"We did an MRI when you were brought in. I'm happy to report that there's no fracture and no hemorrhage in the brain," the doctor said, tucking a loose strand of black curly hair behind her ear and pushing her glasses up on her nose. "You do have a concussion, and the effects of that can last for a while. Expect the headache to linger for the next few days. I can give you some prescription-strength Tylenol to take the edge off the headache, or something stronger if you think you'll need it."

"Prescription-strength Tylenol's fine."

The doctor marked something in her chart. "You were really fortunate, you know. If that bullet had traveled a different trajectory—just a half an inch in any direction—the outcome would have been very different." She tucked her pen in her lab-coat pocket and her clipboard under her arm. "There's really no need to keep you here overnight, assuming there's someone at home to monitor you."

"I'll be with her," Rose piped up.

The doctor looked over at Rose, then back at Laney, an almost indiscernible look of concern crossing her face. "Do you two live alone?"

"Oh, we don't live together," Rose responded. "I like my space. But I'm happy to stay with her for a few days."

"I see." The doctor frowned. "Maybe it *would* be best if you stayed here overnight, Laney." Her gaze jumped to Grayson. "Unless you two—"

"No!" Laney said quickly, cheeks reddening. "He's a—"

"Law enforcement." Grayson cut in.

"I see," the doctor responded. "It's no problem to let you stay here tonight, Laney. We can monitor your condition—"

"I'll be fine, doctor. I'm sure I'll sleep better in my own bed," Laney insisted.

"Well, if you're certain, the nurse will be in momentarily to remove the IV. She'll give you written wound-care instructions and your medication, then wheel you out."

"I think I can make it out without a wheelchair—" Laney began, but the doctor was already walking out of the room, with Deputy Chief Wallace close behind. Grayson figured they would discuss Laney. Though he was curious to know what they were saying, he was more interested in making sure Laney stayed safe, so he didn't follow. He just waited as Rose hovered over Laney, chatting incessantly, while a nurse arrived and removed the IV. Grayson spent the time counting the seconds in his head until he could get Laney safely home.

The nurse handed Laney discharge instructions and a bottle of pills and went to look for a wheelchair.

A few seconds later, Wallace returned. "Looks like you're clear to go, Laney. Once the nurse gets back, I'll roll you out and—"

"How about you take Rose, and I'll take Laney?" Grayson suggested.

"Now, wait just a minute," Rose protested. "I'm staying right here with my niece until she leaves this building."

"Rose," Laney interrupted. "Don't argue. Just do what you're asked so we can get things moving. I want to get out of here quickly, and I don't really care how it happens."

Rose's face softened. "Of course, love. But don't you

worry. I'll have Tommy bring me to your house. I'll be there when you get home." Rose began to turn away but stopped. "Oh, I almost forgot, I brought you some clothes and your spare house keys. They're in the bag on the bed. Do you need help dressing?"

"I'll manage."

"Then I guess I'll see you at home. Come on, Tommy." She grabbed Wallace's arm and dragged him to the door.

"That's your cue to leave, too," Laney told Grayson quietly. She'd regained some of her color, but she still looked too fragile for Grayson's liking. He wasn't completely happy that she was being released tonight. He would have preferred she stay in the hospital under guard until they found the kidnappers, but since that wasn't going to happen, escorting her home was the next best option.

"I thought we agreed that we're going together."

"We may be leaving together, but I'm not putting on my street clothes while you're standing in the room." She reached into the bag Rose had brought and pulled out what looked like a huge pink sweater. "Great," she muttered.

"Don't like the color choice?"

She turned the sweater so he could see the front. A giant white poodle with fuzzy yarn fur stared out at him.

"Nice," he said, swallowing a laugh.

"If she brought me the matching leggings…" She pulled out bright pink leggings covered in white dog bones. "She did."

"A Christmas gift?"

"Birthday. Two years ago. Needless to say, I've never worn them. Typical Rose, bringing them for me when she knows I have no other option but to put them on."

Grayson smirked. He wasn't into fashion, but even he could see why a person would not want to be caught dead in that getup.

Then the smirk died on his lips, the thought sobering

him instantly. The truth was that if he wasn't vigilant, that is exactly what could happen to Laney Kensington.

"You have options," he said. "It's that or the hospital gown. Pick your poison."

"Right." She pulled the outfit to her chest. "I'll change in the bathroom."

It took her longer than it should have. She might have told the doctor she was feeling okay, but Grayson wasn't buying it. Her eyes had been glassy, her complexion still a little too waxy. If she passed out in the bathroom, he wouldn't know it.

"Laney?" Grayson rapped on the door. "You okay?"

"Fine." She opened the door, her body covered from neck to ankle in pink and white.

He shouldn't have smiled. He knew it, but he couldn't stop himself.

"Wow," he murmured as she met his gaze.

"And not in a good way, right?"

"You almost make it work."

She offered a wan smile and sighed. "I'm not worried about making it work. I'm worried about everyone in the hospital catching a glimpse of me in it. If we're trying to slip out of here undetected, this outfit isn't going to help."

"I can fix that," Grayson said, shrugging out of his jacket and setting it on her shoulders. She slipped her arms into the sleeves, and he tugged the hood up over her hair, his fingers grazing silky skin.

That he noticed surprised him. Since Andrea's death, he'd devoted himself to his job. There wasn't room in his life for anything else.

He stepped back. The jacket hung past Laney's thighs, the sleeves covering her hands.

"It's a little big," he said.

She scowled, pulling at the pink leggings. "Not big enough, I'm afraid."

He laughed. "Well, at least the poodle is covered."

"There is that." She grabbed Aunt Rose's bag from the bed. "Do you think if I press the button, the nurse will come any faster? I'm ready to get out of here."

"You can give it a try," he responded. He was anxious to leave, too. He had an uneasy feeling that said things weren't going to go down as smoothly as he wanted them to.

Laney jabbed the call button. "Really, I think a wheelchair is silly. I'm perfectly capable of—"

The lights went out, the room plunging into darkness. No light seeping in under the door. No light filtering in from behind the curtain. When he'd driven in, Grayson had noticed construction signs for a new wing—perhaps the power outage was related to that. Unfortunately, he couldn't afford to assume anything.

"What's going on?" Laney whispered.

"I don't know," he responded, grabbing her hand and pulling her close to his side. "But, I can tell you this. We're not waiting for the wheelchair."

FOUR

Laney's nerves were on edge, her vision adjusting to the darkness as Agent DeMarco guided her toward the door. It flew open as they reached it, and Detective Jensen barged in. The door slammed shut behind him. "What do you make of this, DeMarco?" His voice was low and tense. His hand rested on his holstered revolver.

"Could be a power outage from the construction that's going on or—" the agent glanced at Laney "—something less innocuous. It's hard to say, but I don't like it. We need to get Laney out of here."

"You have a plan for doing that without attracting too much attention?"

"Laney and I will leave now, through the hospital service entrance on the ground floor. I'll take care of getting her home. You call Chief Andrews and fill him in. We're going to need a couple of guys down here to investigate— we need to know for sure what caused this outage."

"Do you really think this power failure could be connected to the kidnapping?" Laney interjected. "It seems like that would be a lot of trouble to go through."

"How much trouble is too much trouble if it's going to keep a multimillion-dollar operation running?" Agent DeMarco asked.

It was a good question. One that Laney couldn't answer.

Agent DeMarco struck her as levelheaded and calculated, completely focused on the investigation. If he thought the hospital's power failure could be staged by the kidnappers, she wouldn't write off the idea.

"Are you sure you don't need me for backup?" Detective Jensen asked, brows furrowed in concern.

"I'd rather you stand your post. Act like you're still guarding the room. Make note of everyone that comes by—hospital employee, electrician, patient—everyone," Agent DeMarco replied.

"Will do." Detective Jensen pulled the door open, stepping out of the way, and Agent DeMarco pressed a warm hand to the small of Laney's back.

"Stay close," he said as he led her into the hall.

She didn't need the reminder. She planned on staying glued to his side until they exited the building. The emergency generator must have turned on. The hallway wasn't quite as dark as the room had been. A row of red lights illuminated the area, providing just enough light to see down the corridor to the dimly glowing exit sign.

A nurse made her way down the corridor, peeking into rooms as she went, calling reassurances to patients, inquiring about the occupants' welfare. Other than that, the hallway was empty, the stillness of the hospital unsettling. Agent DeMarco took Laney's elbow, urging her toward the stairwell.

"We're going to have to take the stairs," he said, wrapping his arm around her waist, pulling her closer to his side, the protective gesture somehow reassuring. "We're on the eighth floor, do you think you'll be able to make it?"

"Yes, I'll be fine." She didn't have a choice.

"If you need to take a break, let me know. If you get dizzy or—"

"How about we just go?" she cut him off, because the longer they stood around talking, the more her head ached and the less energy her legs seemed to have. They were on the eighth floor, which meant navigating seven flights of stairs down to the ground floor. She was fit and healthy. She had to be to train dogs the way she did. On most days, she could sprint up ten flights of stairs and barely break a sweat. This wasn't most days.

"Just remember," he responded, opening the stairwell door and ushering her onto the landing, "you pass out and I'll be carrying you out of here like a sack of potatoes, not worrying about maintaining your dignity."

"If I pass out, dignity won't be first on my priority list."

But neither of them would have to worry about it, because there was no way she was passing out in the stairwell like some damsel in distress. That wasn't her style. It was bad enough she was forced to make a covert escape from the hospital in tight, itchy leggings and a fuzzy poodle sweater. She wasn't going to do it lying over Agent DeMarco's shoulder.

Not if she could help it.

By the time they reached the fifth-floor landing, she wasn't sure she could.

Her head throbbed with almost every jarring step. She was dizzy and nauseated. The only thing that kept her on her feet was the horrifying vision of herself slung over Agent DeMarco's shoulder, her puffy sweater–clad torso slapping into his back as he jogged down the stairs.

Just five more flights of stairs. Four more. She counted them off in her head, forcing herself to take one step after another. She'd do everything she needed to do to buy the FBI and the MPD some time if that meant there was a chance of finding Olivia and the other children.

Her feet seemed leaden, every step more difficult than the one before, but she kept going, because she didn't want the image of Olivia's fear-filled eyes to be the last one she had of the girl. She wanted to see photos of her being reunited with her family, wanted to see her smiling and happy and playing the violin she'd been carrying when she was abducted. She wanted this time to be different. She needed a happy ending for Olivia. An ending she'd not been able to offer her teammates' families…

She stumbled, her legs nearly giving out.

Agent DeMarco's grip tightened on her waist. "Do you need to sit for a minute?" His voice rumbled close to her ear, his breath ruffling the fine hairs near her temple.

"No. I'm fine," she lied, and kept walking.

Laney was lying, and Grayson knew it.

He wouldn't insist she sit down, though. He wanted her out of the hospital, and this stairwell, as quickly as possible. If that meant carrying her out, so be it.

Voices drifted into the stairwell as they neared the third-floor landing. Grayson tensed, wary of who might be approaching. He didn't believe in coincidences, and a power outage at the hospital while the key witness to a kidnapping was in it would be a big one. It was possible the construction crew had knocked out the power, but he wasn't counting on it. If the kidnappers were responsible for the power outage, they might be on a fact-finding mission, hoping to discover who Laney was and whether or not she was actually deceased.

If they already knew she was alive, Grayson had a new problem. Namely that someone who knew Laney had survived had leaked the information to the kidnappers. Though he hoped it wasn't the case, a leak could explain why the kidnappers always seemed one step ahead.

Laney stumbled again. He pulled her closer, steadying her.

"We're almost there," he murmured, leading her down the stairs as quietly as possible. By the time they reached the second floor, she was visibly weak, her hand clutching the railing as she took the final step onto the landing.

Even in the dim red light, he could see the paleness of her skin, the hollows beneath her cheeks. Her eyes were glassy, her skin dewy from perspiration. She might have the will to make it out of the stairwell, but he wasn't sure she had the strength.

He pulled the hood from her head and pressed a palm to her forehead. Her skin was cool and clammy, her breathing shallow and quick. "Maybe you'd better sit for a minute."

She backed away from his touch, squaring her shoulders and yanking the hood back up over her hair. "I appreciate your concern, but if we stop every time I feel light-headed or dizzy, we might not make it out until morning."

Her matter-of-fact tone left no room to argue, so he stayed silent. Now was not the time for a struggle of wills.

"Three more flights to go," he pointed out, and he thought he heard her sigh quietly in response.

It was taking forever to reach ground level, but then, Grayson wasn't the kind of guy who liked to do things slowly. He liked to have a plan in place and execute it with efficiency and as much speed as was prudent.

In this case, that meant going at a snail's pace.

It would have been quicker and easier to carry Laney the rest of the way down, but she wouldn't have appreciated it, and he needed her cooperation.

Somewhere above them, a door opened and shut with a bang.

How many floors above? he wondered. Four? Three?

Grayson stilled, listening. A quick shuffling of feet, then nothing.

Ten seconds passed.

Twenty.

The stairwell remained eerily silent. He didn't like it. Someone was up there, still and listening, and he had a hunch it wasn't a hospital employee. If he was right, his witness's identity had been compromised. Peering over the railing, he scanned the stairwell below, its dark corners untouched by the dim emergency lights. There were now only two flights between them and escape. Multiple doors that the enemy could enter. He and Laney were vulnerable here, sandwiched between whoever had entered above and anyone who might be waiting below.

If there had been any other way out of the hospital, he would have selected it over the stairwell. Experience had taught him stairwells were prime locations for an ambush. A gunman above, a gunman below, and a person could be taken out in an instant.

Caught between floors, they had no choice but to continue down. He doubted Laney would make it up even one flight of stairs. Meeting her eyes, he held a finger to his lips, then guided her quickly down.

On the ground floor below, another door opened. He could hear heavy footsteps coming their way.

Not good.

Grayson had no intention of being caught in the middle of an ambush. Better to go on the offensive—meet trouble one-on-one. Grayson urged Laney down to the first floor landing, gently pushing her into the shadows. Drawing his gun, he peered over the rail.

A shadowy figure ascended the steps quickly, the barrel of a gun glinting in the dim emergency lights. From above, footsteps echoed loudly as the second person rushed down the stairs.

Grayson needed to act now. And it wouldn't be by the book.

If he announced himself, he'd lose the element of surprise. If he took a bullet, Laney would be easy pickings.

There's no way that was happening.

He had to time it perfectly. The gunman slowed as he

neared the landing, cautiously stepping around the corner, gun first. In one quick motion, Grayson cracked the butt of his service weapon on the guy's wrist, eliciting a startled howl of pain and sending the gun clattering down the stairs.

The guy turned back—whether to flee or retrieve his gun, Grayson couldn't be sure. Reaching out, Grayson grasped a handful of the guy's sweatshirt and brought his gun forcefully down on the man's temple. The blow sent the man crumpling to the ground in a motionless heap.

Grabbing Laney's arm, Grayson pulled her forward, ushering her around the fallen assailant. The unmistakable pop of a silenced pistol echoed in the stairwell, a bullet slamming into the concrete wall a foot from Grayson's head. He shoved Laney forward, placing himself between her and the gunman as they raced down the last few steps to ground level.

He shoved the door open, scanning the hallway and the open door of the room beyond. Backup lights illuminated the hospital's laundry room, the huge cavernous area the perfect cover for anyone who might be lying in wait. Footsteps pounded on the stairs above, the second gunman moving in quickly.

Grayson dragged Laney into the hallway, shielding her from any threat that might be waiting.

"This way." He motioned toward a glowing neon exit sign pointing them to their escape route. They ran toward the far wall, turning the corner as the stairwell door slammed open once more.

Grabbing Laney's hand, he sprinted toward the exit. He knew she was struggling to match his pace, but slowing down wasn't an option.

Right now he couldn't worry about anything but getting her to safety—as safe as any place could be for the only witness against a very large, very lucrative crime ring.

They barreled through the exit door into the employee parking lot.

"Come on," he encouraged her. "I parked my car out here."

Agent DeMarco didn't let go of Laney's hand as they ran through a near-empty parking lot. Silver streaks of moonlight managed to break through the intermittent cloud cover, providing some visibility beyond the shadows of the building. Too much visibility if their pursuer ran out of the building behind them. Laney shuddered at the thought.

She didn't want to be within sight of that door if it opened and the gunman appeared.

Her body was wearing down, though. No matter how much she wanted to keep sprinting along beside Agent DeMarco, she wasn't sure how much farther she could go. Her legs shook, every pounding step across the pavement making her head throb.

She stumbled, and his grip on her hand tightened.

"You can do this," he urged her.

Maybe she could.

If wherever they were heading was closer than a few steps.

They rounded the corner of the building, putting brick and mortar between themselves and the door. She wanted to feel safer because of it, but fear pulsed through her veins, churned in her stomach. They had no idea how many men were after them—or where their attackers might be lying in wait.

A sudden clatter from around the building, like a can kicked across pavement, had Agent DeMarco snagging the arm of the jacket she wore, yanking her behind a large metal Dumpster.

"Stay hidden. I'll be right back," he ordered before easing around the Dumpster and moving soundlessly into the night. She stood still, keeping as quiet as possible. Listening. She could hear nothing but the deafening rush of her own blood in her ears. Without Agent DeMarco, she felt exposed and vulnerable. Releasing the breath she hadn't realized she was holding, she tried to shake off that feeling.

She'd worked under stressful, even dangerous, circumstances in the past, and she'd never had to rely on anyone to get her through them. She couldn't allow herself to rely on Agent DeMarco, either. Playing the part of the victim just wasn't her style. After all, if something happened to him, she would have to take care of herself.

And she would. She'd been doing it her whole life.

She'd realized at age eight that her mom was powerless to protect either of them from her father's violent outbursts. Laney had been forced to take on that role. She'd learned to protect them both. This was no different. She needed to be ready. She needed to assess the situation herself. Plan her escape route should anything go wrong.

She eased out from behind the Dumpster, peering into the darkness. Nothing. The night seemed too still, the parking lot too dark. Dozens of cars were there, the streetlights off, the moon temporarily hidden by clouds.

A shadow moved at the edge of the lot, a deeper darkness in the gloom.

She jerked back, heart pounding wildly.

"Good choice," someone whispered, and she jumped, spinning toward the voice.

Big mistake. Blood rushed from her head, and she swayed.

Firm hands cupped her waist, held her steady as she caught her balance.

She looked into Agent DeMarco's face. "Where did you come from?" she whispered.

"I was circling around to get a location on him. I also told you to stay out of sight."

"I did."

"You didn't." His hands dropped away. "I had you in a position of cover. You walked out where anyone could see you."

"It's dark."

"Ever heard of night-vision goggles?" he asked. "Because someone who has money enough to run a kidnapping ring the size of the one we're dealing with has money for all kinds of things the average Joe might not have at his disposal."

She hadn't thought about that, but she wasn't going to admit it.

"Did you see him?" she asked.

"He's headed in the other direction—toward the visitor's parking lot, but it won't take him long to figure out we're not there and double back." He grabbed her arm, leading her toward the parking lot. "Come on. Let's not lose our head start."

FIVE

The investigation had been compromised, and Grayson needed to find out who was responsible. But first, he needed to get Laney as far away from the gunman as possible.

He'd already called the local PD. Officers would be on the scene soon. They could deal with the gunmen. Grayson would deal with protecting Laney.

"You live in Davidsonville, right?" Grayson asked, laying his cell phone in the center console.

"Yes." Laney glanced over at him. "The quickest way is Route 50 to the 424 exit—that road is a straight shot to my community."

"I don't think we'll go the quickest route," he said as he stopped at the darkened signal lights on Hospital Drive. He'd seen the gunman moving through the parking lot, could have taken a shot at him, but he had no idea how many others there might be, and he couldn't afford to take any chances.

"Why not? The sooner we get home, the happier I'll be," Laney responded, leaning forward in her seat, scanning the darkness as if watching could keep trouble from coming.

"I don't want to risk anyone following us." He turned left on the main road, heading away from her house.

She looked over her shoulder, eyeing the empty road. "I hadn't thought about that."

"Then, it's good we're together," he responded. "Because anyone who'd take a couple of shots at someone while she's with an FBI agent isn't going to hesitate to follow us."

"He might not have known who you were."

"Maybe not." But Grayson thought the perp did. Whoever the kidnappers were, they seemed well connected. Somehow, some way, they'd found out that Laney was alive.

"But you think he did?" she asked.

"I don't know, but I'm not willing to take chances with your life."

"What about Olivia's? If the kidnappers know I'm alive, they may move her now. If they're desperate enough, they may do worse."

He'd had the same thought. He didn't like it any more than Laney seemed to. "She's a high-priced commodity. I doubt they'll do anything that will compromise their bottom line."

"You doubt it, but you don't know," Laney said with a sigh. "I should have—"

"You should have stayed behind the Dumpster when I left you there." He cut her off, because he understood the regrets she had, the guilt. They wouldn't do Olivia any good. They wouldn't do Laney any good, either.

"We've covered this ground before," she responded wearily.

"And now we'll cover it again. I need you to understand what we're dealing with. You have to listen to the precautions I suggest and take them seriously."

"I understand…"

"I don't think you do. You're my only witness, Laney. The key to closing a case I've been pursuing for over a year."

"Wow," she said drily. "I feel so…special."

That surprised a laugh out of him. After speaking with

Andrews, he'd known Laney was a force to be reckoned with. He hadn't expected her to make him smile, though. "You should. I gave you my coat. I'm taking you for a moonlit drive."

"You're saving my life," she added quietly.

"You saved your own life. Or maybe Murphy did. You'll have to thank him." He glanced in the rearview mirror. Nothing. No sign that they were being followed. He wasn't sure that meant anything. If the perps knew their witness was alive, they might also know her identity. He drove into a cul-de-sac, waited a few seconds, drove out again. Still no sign of a tail.

His phone vibrated, and he answered it quickly. "De-Marco here."

"It's Kent Andrews. I'm at the hospital."

"What'd you find?"

"No sign of either of the perps. The fire marshal is here assessing the damage from the electrical fire that caused the power outage. He's calling in the arson investigator. Looks like the wiring in the circuit panel was tampered with. Someone went through a lot of trouble to make it look like faulty wiring, but the fire chief isn't buying it. How's Laney doing?"

Grayson glanced at Laney.

She smiled, and something in his heart stirred to life, some gut-level, knee-jerk reaction that surprised him as much as his laughter had. "I'll let her answer," he responded.

That was Laney's cue to speak, and it should have been easy enough to answer Kent's question. The problem was, she wasn't sure how she was doing.

"Laney?" Kent prodded.

"I'm fine," she managed, and Kent let out a bark of laughter.

"You were shot in the head. You're not fine."

"In a couple of days, I think I'll be good as new."

"That's a relief," he said, "You had us all worried. Murphy was beside himself, by the way. Wouldn't let anyone near you, even the patrolman who responded to the scene. Luckily he was wearing his MPD collar, so a K-9 handler was called in. He backed down on command." Laney could hear the smile in Kent's voice. "He did real good tonight."

"Yes, he did." She smiled at the thought of the overly excitable dog, of the hours she'd spent working with him, determined to make him into the K-9 team member she thought he could be. She hadn't been sure it would work. Not every dog was capable of the focus required, and Murphy had already flunked out of the K-9 training program once. Now there was hope. All the hard work on both their parts was finally paying off. "Where is he now?"

"He's at headquarters being pampered. The guys bought him a huge steak and brought a dog bed into the office for him. He thinks he's a king or something. Never seen that dog look quite so proud of himself."

Laney laughed. "Good for him." Before tonight, you couldn't have paid a K-9 handler to work with Murphy. A couple more weeks and he'd be ready to enter the program again.

"We'll take good care of him until you're ready to have him back. Don't you worry."

"You can bring him by tomorrow. I don't want any breaks in his training routine. He's almost there."

"Are you sure? Wallace reported back the doctor's orders for you to take it easy for a few days." The concern in Kent's voice was obvious. The guy was gruff and abrupt most of the time, but he had a heart of gold.

"I won't overdo it. Riley and Bria both work tomorrow, so I'll have plenty of help at the kennel."

"You're not going there tomorrow," Agent DeMarco said so abruptly, she nearly jumped out of her seat belt.

"Going where?"

"To the kennel."

"Of course I am. It's my job."

"You think your job is worth dying over?" DeMarco responded, and Laney frowned, all her fatigue washed away by a wave of irritation mixed with anxiety.

"Of course not, but I have to live my life."

"Have your crew do the work at the kennel tomorrow," Kent cut in. "That will be the safer. As a matter of fact, maybe you should be in a safe house until we find the guys who are after you. What do you think, DeMarco?"

A safe house?

Laney hadn't even given that scenario a thought. She'd agreed she wouldn't take unnecessary chances, but she wasn't sure she was willing to put her life on hold. After all, if the kidnappers knew who she was, they could have just waited for her to arrive home rather than cause an elaborate power outage at the hospital.

"I think we can wait on that," Agent DeMarco responded. "If the kidnappers knew her identity, they would have waited at her place, taken her out there." Hearing her own thoughts spoken aloud, imagining men skulking in the shadows of her house, made her blood go cold.

"Are you sure waiting is the best decision, DeMarco?" Kent asked.

"No. But I *am* sure there's a leak, and since I don't know if it's in my house or yours, I can't be certain Laney will be any more protected in a safe house than she would be at her own house, under guard."

"Okay. I'll send an officer over. He'll be there when you arrive.

"Thanks, Andrews."

"Laney's one of us. We'll do whatever's needed to keep her safe."

"Understood. When do you think you'll be wrapping things up over there?"

"About an hour. We're waiting for copies of the surveillance video and questioning the security guard."

"Did he see anyone in the area?"

"He says he didn't." Laney could hear the hesitation in Kent's voice.

"But you're not buying it?" Grayson asked.

"It's just a gut feeling, but no." Kent said. "We're going to make an excuse to get him down to the precinct for more thorough questioning."

"I think I'll get someone to run a background check on the guy. Can you email me his information?" Grayson asked.

"Sure, but the hospital does a thorough background check before they hire someone. I think you'll find that his record's clean."

"I'm more interested in the state of his bank account."

"You think he was hired to set that fire—or look the other way?" Kent asked, his Boston accent thicker than usual. He'd transplanted from New England years ago, but Laney had noticed that the faster he talked and the more enthused he was about the subject, the thicker the accent became.

"I just want to be thorough," Agent DeMarco replied.

"And yet, you didn't ask me about his work record."

"I take it you checked?"

"Absolutely," the chief said, sounding almost gleeful. "His logs check out, but he's been reprimanded previously for sleeping on the job. Ideally the surveillance videos will give us a good look at what really transpired while he was on duty tonight."

"I like the way you think, Andrews," DeMarco said as

he veered onto Route 50. "Do you mind if I drop by the precinct while you're questioning the guard?"

"That's not a problem."

"Then I'll head over after I get Laney settled."

"See you then." Kent disconnected, and Laney laid her head back against the seat, tempted to close her eyes just for a minute. She was that tired. So tired she didn't care that she might start snoring loudly while a good-looking FBI agent sat beside her.

"You still with me?" Agent DeMarco asked.

"Where else would I be?"

"Dreaming?"

"Good idea. I think I'll give it a try," she responded, and then she did exactly what she'd been wanting to do, closed her eyes, the pain still pulsing through her head as DeMarco sped along the highway.

Grayson found Wynwood easily, driving into Laney's well-established, affluent neighborhood and glancing in his rearview mirror as he turned onto her street.

Nothing. The road was empty. Just the way he wanted it.

Laney groaned softly, asleep, but obviously not pain-free.

He didn't wake her. Just followed his GPS coordinates down the quiet street. Grand brick homes sat far back from the street, their large lots sporting well-manicured lawns and decorative plants. Nothing wild or unkempt about this place. People who lived here were affluent and not afraid to show it.

It was a nice community. Pretty. Well-planned.

Laney shifted in her seat, and he glanced her way. She'd pulled his jacket close, her hands barely peeking out of rolled cuffs. It reminded him of a spring evening long ago, the scent of rain in the air, the refreshing coolness. Reminded him of Andrea, her senior year of college, his jacket around her shoulders as they lay on a blanket watching the sunset. He'd proposed to her that day, and she'd had the tiny diamond ring, the best he could afford, on her finger.

"Our access road is on the right, just after that set of mailboxes," Laney said, her voice rough with sleep. It jarred him from memories that he tried hard not to dwell on.

The past was what it was. He couldn't change it.

He could only move forward, do everything in his power to be the man God wanted him to be, do the work that had been set before him.

"Where?" He could see nothing but thick foliage that butted up against the narrowing road. This end of the neighborhood had fewer houses and was less polished, but there was beauty in the overgrown fields that stretched out on either side of the road.

"See those tall bushes?" She gestured to the left. "And the mailboxes? Just slow to a crawl. You'll see the access road when you're almost on top of it."

He did as she suggested, barely coasting past the mailboxes until he spotted the road, a long gravel driveway lined with mature trees.

He drove nearly a quarter of a mile down the gravel road before the first house appeared. A quaint one-story cottage with white shutters and a wraparound porch, it was nothing like the other houses in the neighborhood. The moon had edged out from behind the clouds, its reflected light shimmering across a small pond set off to the left. Tall trees cast dark shadows across the gardens and neatly cut yard surrounding the building—perfect hiding places for an assailant. Despite his confidence that they'd not been followed from the hospital, Grayson wasn't comfortable with this setup at all.

"Perfect," he muttered under his breath, imagining all the ways someone could approach the house unnoticed.

"It really is," Laney agreed. Apparently she hadn't heard the sarcasm in his voice. "My great-grandfather built it. At one time, he owned all the land in the neighborhood. When my grandfather sold a portion of the land, he kept the cottage and the main house. Aunt Rose lives in the cottage. I'm at the main house."

"Which is where?" he asked. The location of the cottage wasn't ideal. Maybe the main house was in a less secluded spot.

"Just keep following the driveway. It veers past the cottage. The house is another quarter mile in."

The headlights of the sedan flashed across thick woods and heavy foliage as Grayson drove past the cottage.

The "main house," as Laney had called it, looked to be a slightly larger version of Rose's cottage. Same wooden shingles, same white shutters and a very similar porch. Its single-story layout meant that all rooms of the house could be easily accessed by an intruder. Worse, it sat in the middle of a clearing that looked to be approximately twenty acres in diameter and was surrounded by woods on three sides, making it a surveillance nightmare.

Grayson pulled up to Laney's darkened home and turned off the engine. "What's in the back of the house?"

"The kennels, agility course and covered training pavilion." Laney tried unsuccessfully to suppress a yawn. "Would you like a cup of coffee before you head out?" she asked.

"I'll pass on the coffee, but let me take a quick look around the property while I wait for the officer to arrive."

"Sure. I'll turn on the outside lights for you."

"Hold on," he said, but she was already opening the door and stepping out of the car.

By the time Grayson had grabbed his flashlight from

the glove box and exited his vehicle, Laney was halfway up the stone walkway to her house. For someone who'd nearly died, she moved fast, making her way up the porch stairs. He wasn't sure how long it would take her to realize she didn't have the bag her aunt had packed for her. Rose had said the keys were in it, so he grabbed it, heading up the porch steps after her.

She was patting the pocket of his jacket as he reached her side. The hood had fallen off her head, and her auburn hair looked glossy black in the darkness, her face a pale oval. "I hope I didn't leave my keys at the hospital," she said, plucking at the fuzzy sweater as if the keys might be hiding in there.

"Didn't Rose mention she'd put your spare set in the bag?" He held it out, and she took it, offering a smile that made her look young and a little vulnerable.

"Oh, that's right. Thanks." She dug the keys out, said good-night and walked inside. Seconds later, the porch light went on, casting a soft white glow across most of the yard. He saw the front curtains part slightly and wondered if it was Rose or Laney who peeked out.

He waved to whoever it was, then turned toward the yard. A large sign sat to the left of the driveway. He flashed his light across it, reading Wagging Tails Boarding and Training Facility. Flower beds around the sign and in front of the house were similar to those surrounding Rose's cottage. A cool breeze carried the faint scent of pine and honeysuckle. Above the sound of the rustling wind, Grayson detected the crunching of leaves and underbrush in the woods to the left of the house. He turned the corner of the house just in time to see the last of a small herd of deer returning to the safety of the woods.

He trained his flashlight back toward the house, inspecting the grass and mulch beds for signs of disturbance. Nothing.

The window screens were all in place. Floodlights shimmered over the expanse of yard between the house and the kennels. He was impressed by the setup. There was a very large agility course with tunnels, beams, ladders, hoops, cones and platforms at various heights connected by tight netting. The kennel looked as if it could accommodate twenty dogs, with each dog having its own inside space and an exterior fenced-in run. The dogs were in for the night. One or two barked as he walked around the structure, checking doors. Everything was locked.

Next to the kennel, the covered pavilion was also fenced in. He walked around the training facilities, shining his flashlight into the darker corners of the yard and toward the woods. All was quiet. Peaceful. Almost idyllic.

Satisfied that there was no one lurking in the shadows, Grayson turned back toward the house. Laney was safe, at least for the moment. Yet he felt uneasy at the thought of leaving her alone, even for a quick trip to the precinct. He tried to shrug it off. She wasn't in protective custody. At this point, there were limits to what he could do to keep her safe. But Grayson was used to pushing the boundaries, and he knew that if he wanted to solve this case, bring the kids home, and keep Laney safe, he was going to have to think outside the box to do it.

He wasn't sure what that would mean, what it would look like, but he knew one thing for sure—he would do anything necessary to protect his only witness.

SIX

Agent DeMarco was still outside. Laney could see his light bouncing along the tree line near the kennels.

Jax, her six-year-old Australian shepherd, and Brody, her ten-year-old Belgian Malinois, were too happy to see her to notice the stranger out in the yard. Both followed her through the kitchen, tails wagging as they waited patiently for her to acknowledge them. She took off Agent DeMarco's jacket, tossed it over the back of a wooden chair and called the dogs over. They sat in front of her, tails thumping as she scratched behind their ears, murmured a few words of praise. Both barked as a car pulled into the drive. Must be the officer Kent had sent over. That would mean that Agent DeMarco would be heading out soon.

Good. There was something about him that made her... uncomfortable.

Maybe it was the way he studied her, as if she were the secret to some great mystery he had to solve.

She almost laughed at the thought, because that's probably exactly what she was to him.

The only witness to Olivia's kidnapping, the one person who could identify the kidnappers and potentially help put them behind bars.

She tugged at the itchy sweater as she headed toward her bedroom. She needed to take off this getup. Now. Not only because it looked ridiculous but also because it was probably the most uncomfortable outfit she'd ever owned. There was definitely wool in the sweater. Perhaps if she threw it in the washer and then put it through the dryer on high, it would shrink so badly it that wouldn't be fit for anything but the Goodwill bag. She smiled at the thought, but who was she kidding? Even the homeless wouldn't grab this outfit off the rack. The dogs followed her down the hall toward her bedroom.

The door to the guest room at the end of the hall opened, and Aunt Rose popped her head out. "Oh, you're home, dear. Don't you look nice."

Laney ignored the compliment. Aunt Rose meant well, but she had questionable taste at times. "It's after eleven, Aunt Rose. You didn't have to wait up for me."

"I was just catching up on my devotional," Rose said. "Let me grab my slippers and robe and I'll be right out."

"There's really no need…" But Rose shut the guest room door before Laney could get her sentence out. She sighed, hurrying into her room before Rose could reappear. She immediately peeled off the offending tights and sweater, letting them drop to a heap on the floor, then changed into some comfortable yoga pants and her old University of Colorado sweatshirt. A glance in the mirror showed she still had a few faint streaks of blood on one side of her face, and the bruise on her jaw was starting to turn from red to blue. She carefully peeled back the bandage. A thin line of five staples started at her temple, disappearing into the hairline. Only about a half inch of the scar would be visible when healed. The rest would be concealed by her hair.

A shadow passed outside her bedroom room window, and Brody growled deep in his throat. Laney's pulse quickened—then she shook her head, chastising herself for being so jumpy. Agent DeMarco had probably decided to take another look around. She pulled back the curtain, peering out the window. There was no sign of him. Or anyone else.

"It's okay, boy." Brody had always had a protective streak in him—surprising since he had failed his temperament test for the Secret Service as a puppy. Too laid back, they'd said.

She'd been under contract with the company that supplied the puppies and had been given first choice for adoption. She'd seen the potential in him and had turned him into a top-notch search dog, cross-trained in both air scent and human remains detection. He was her first partner. In the years they'd worked together, they'd logged more than a hundred searches in the Colorado wilderness and had twenty-eight live finds to their credit. His hips forced him into early retirement at the age of six. By then, Jax was already trained and operational as an air scent dog. She'd worked exclusively with Jax then, only retiring him after the accident—and before he was able to complete his human-remains detection training.

She knew both dogs missed the work, so she regularly ran training exercises on the weekends with the neighborhood children. That training was all the "action" any of them saw these days. She hadn't been on a real search since that last find. The one that left three teammates dead.

Shaking off the thought, she went into her bathroom, ran a comb through her hair and scrubbed traces of blood from her face.

The doorbell rang, and she hurried to the foyer. Both dogs barked three times and remained at her heel—their signal for a visitor. Laney pointed to the cushions in the corner of the family room, as customary when visitors arrived, and gave the command "place." The dogs immediately sat, eyes trained on Laney, waiting for the next command. She peered out the peephole, saw Agent De-

Marco standing on the porch and opened the door. "I take it everything's clear?" she asked.

He nodded, his eyes scanning the room before his gaze settled on her. "You changed." He smiled, and she was drawn to the dimple at the corner of his mouth. "That look suits you." Her face warmed under his scrutiny. For once, a quick comeback failed her.

"Don't you have a security system out here?"

Laney gestured toward the dogs. "There's my security system."

"Dogs are a great deterrent, but I'd feel a whole lot better if you had a top-notch alarm." He turned, inspecting the deadbolt on the front door.

"It would be a waste of money, Agent DeMarco. Aside from some recent vandalism and petty theft in Wynwood, we've never had much crime out here. It's a long walk down that access road in the dark, and we'd hear a car coming up the gravel drive before it could reach us."

"A walk down the gravel driveway in the dark versus announcing their presence and a lifetime in prison? How do you think a criminal would weigh that?"

"Point taken."

Grayson turned his attention back to her. "I see the bandage is gone."

He closed the small gap between them.

"Do you mind if I look?" he asked, gesturing to her temple.

She shook her head, and then he was in her space, and she was breathing the fresh scent of the outdoors mixed with something dark and undeniably masculine. "Go ahead," she responded, her voice just a little rougher than she wanted it to be.

He gently lifted her hair, his warm fingers lightly brushing her forehead. Laney's cheeks heated as he studied the wound.

Finally, he let her hair drop back into place. "The scar shouldn't be very noticeable once it heals."

"I'm not worried about it. I'm alive. That's way better than the alternative."

"Agreed." He smiled, absently fingering the scar on his left brow.

Had he received it in the line of duty, or was it a battle scar from some childhood antic? She didn't know him well enough to ask, but neither scenario would surprise her. He seemed determined and relentless. Those traits were likely to get a kid into all kinds of trouble.

"But I've found that women can be a little more self-conscious about scars on their faces than most of the men I know," he said.

She shrugged. "We all have scars. Some just run deeper or are more visible than others."

She took a seat on the overstuffed, well-worn leather reclining chair that still smelled of her grandfather's cherry tobacco. She breathed in the scent. Felt herself calming at the memories of him. This home, and her grandfather, had often been her refuge as a child, avoiding her father's drunken rages and her mother's frequent bouts of depression. In her teens, she'd spent more time at her granddad's house, helping him with the kennels and the dog training, than she'd spent in her own home. His passing last year had left a void no one could fill.

Laney looked at the dogs, who were eyeing Agent DeMarco with interest. "The dogs want to say hello. Do you mind?"

"Not at all. I love dogs."

Laney gave a quick hand signal with the word "break." At her command, both dogs bounded off their pillows and headed over to Agent DeMarco, tails wagging. He smiled, rubbing them behind the ears.

"The Aussie is Jax, and the Mal is Brody."

"They're great."

"Thanks." Laney smiled. "They love attention—they'll sit there all night as long as they're getting petted. Do you have a dog?"

"No." Agent DeMarco smiled. "I've thought about getting one, but the truth is, I work too much. It wouldn't be fair to leave it home alone all the time."

"Dogs do need companionship."

"Laney!" Rose called. "Is someone here?"

She had to know someone was. Despite her age, she had perfect hearing. "Yes. We're in the living room."

"Who is it?" Rose asked, sashaying into the room wearing a fuzzy teal robe and a muted pink granny nightgown. Laney might have believed that she'd just rolled out of bed and hurried down the hall, but every hair on Rose's head was in place. She had powder on her cheeks and pink lipstick on her lips. She smiled sweetly as she spotted Agent DeMarco. "Oh, I didn't know you were here, Gray."

"I was looking around outside and decided I'd check in before I left."

"Would you like a cup of tea?"

"No, thank you. I'll be heading out in a minute."

"Maybe you could give Aunt Rose a ride back to her place?" All Laney wanted to do was get in bed and fall asleep. She definitely did not need Aunt Rose flitting about, making herself "useful." As much as she loved Aunt Rose, the woman had more energy than three people combined, and Laney wasn't sure she could handle that tonight.

"What?" Rose responded with a frown. "I'm staying here tonight, remember?"

"There's no need. I don't plan on doing anything but sleeping. I'm sure you'd be more comfortable in your own bed."

"Well, that's a thought, but it's not going to happen," Rose said, grabbing the bag from the foyer floor as she entered the family room. "You heard what the doctor said—you shouldn't be alone for a few days."

"The doctor was speaking out of an abundance of caution."

"She was speaking out of genuine concern for your well-being!"

"I agree with Rose," Agent DeMarco interjected.

"And that's supposed to make me concede?" Laney asked, shooting him a sideways look.

"I once knew a man who got knocked in the head by a piece of shrapnel," Agent DeMarco said. "He thought he was fine until he wasn't."

"If you're going to tell me he keeled over and died, I'm not going to believe you."

"I was going to tell you that he ended up in the hospital in a coma for two weeks, but your version is a lot more compelling."

If she hadn't been so tired, if her head hadn't been aching so badly, she might have smiled at that.

"That's settled, then," Rose stated matter-of-factly. "There is no way I'm leaving you here and having you fall into a coma. You look a little flushed. Have you taken your painkiller yet?"

"No, I haven't had a chance. I'll take some in a minute."

"You'll take some now." Rose rifled through the bag, pulling out the bottle of pills. "I'll get a glass of water. Stay put." She hurried off.

Which left Laney and Agent DeMarco alone in the family room.

That should have been fine. She was used to being around male law enforcement officers.

But it felt odd having him there, eyeing her somberly.

"What?" she finally asked.

"I got word that the sketch artist flies in at one-fifteen

tomorrow. I'll have her here between two and three, depending on traffic."

"That seems a long time to wait…"

"She's worth the wait. The best in the nation." Agent DeMarco studied her. She felt her face flush under his scrutiny. "Are you sure you're going to be up to working with her?"

"I'd work with her now if I could."

"Just take care of yourself between now and then."

"You've got to make sure your key witness stays healthy, huh?" she joked. Only Agent DeMarco didn't look like he thought it was funny.

"I need to make sure *you* stay healthy," he responded. "You're important to my case, but you're also a civilian, and it's my job to make sure you stay safe."

"It's not—"

He held up a hand. "It's late. You need to rest, and I've got to meet Andrews at the precinct. Stay inside. Don't leave the house for any reason—not to walk the dogs, not to run to the grocery store, not to check the mail. Not for anything."

Having never been one who liked to be told what to do, Laney tried to control her annoyance at his demanding tone. She'd been making her own decisions since she was eight and was accustomed to weighing her options and deciding the best course of action for herself. In the end, she was the one who had to deal with the consequences of her choices. "Agent DeMarco, I appreciate your concern, but…"

"Call me Grayson, or Gray. Your aunt already took the liberty, so it only seems fitting that you do as well."

"Fine, Grayson. I appreciate your concern, but let's not forget there's an officer parked right outside."

"Don't be lulled into a false sense of security. Remember, if someone manages to get to you, they'll get to your aunt, too."

He had a point, and she'd be foolish not to consider it. If

something happened to Laney, if she was shot or wounded or attacked, Aunt Rose would run out to help. "Okay. I'll stay close to home." She had a few board-and-trains in the kennel, but that was a short walk from the house.

"Glad to hear it." His gaze jumped to a point beyond her shoulder, and he smiled. "You're just in time, Rose. I've got to head out of here."

"I found your jacket hanging over a chair in the kitchen." Rose handed it over. "And Laney's business card is in the pocket. Just in case you need to reach her."

"Aunt Rose!" Laney protested, but Grayson was already walking out the door, pulling it firmly shut behind him.

She crossed to the window and pulled back the curtain just enough to peek outside. She felt foolish doing it, like a teenager mooning over a secret crush, but she still watched him stop and chat with the officer before getting in the car, anyway. Her work cell phone buzzed, but she ignored it. Probably Kent checking in on her.

It buzzed again, and she sighed, letting the curtain drop and grabbing the phone from the coffee table. She had two text messages from a number she didn't recognize. Curious, she opened the first one. Get away from the window, and save this number in your contacts. Gray.

The second one said, See you tomorrow afternoon.

That made her smile. She was still smiling as she said good-night to Rose and headed to her room.

SEVEN

Laney usually slept with her windows open in the early fall, but after Grayson's warnings, she thought it best to keep them closed. It was nearly midnight by the time she pulled the comforter around her and lowered her head onto her soft down pillow. She closed her eyes against the dull ache in her temple. Even after Rose had retired to the spare room and the house had grown quiet, Laney found herself shifting restlessly in her bed, sleep evading her despite her exhaustion. It seemed like hours before she was finally lulled to sleep by the soft breathing of her dogs.

She woke with a start, blood rushing loudly in her ears with every beat of her heart. She lay still, trying to control her breathing, listening for some sign of what had yanked her from her sleep. The silence was deafening. Pale silver moonlight streamed in through a sliver of an opening in the curtains, casting its eerie glow across her bedroom walls and floor. The blue numbers on her digital alarm clock announced the time as two-fifteen.

Suddenly Brody emitted a low growl. Rising from his spot on the floor, hackles up, he walked toward the window. Soon Jax was beside him, a silent sentry focused on the window. A small scraping sound caught her attention— like a tree branch brushing softly against the screen or the siding. But there were no trees outside her window.

Was someone there? A dark shadow outside the window blocked the moon's light for a brief instant, and she knew. Something—or someone—*was* there.

She grabbed her cell phone, hands shaking as she found Grayson's number and dialed. He picked up on the first ring.

"Grayson?" Laney whispered. "It's Laney."

"Laney." His voice was instantly alert. "What is it?"

"I'm not sure." Her voice trembled as she tried to keep from being heard by whoever was out there. "The dogs are growling, and I thought I saw a shadow pass by my window." She paused, listening. "I'll admit I'm a little on edge after tonight, so I might be overreacting... It could just be the officer looking around. Should I go check?"

"No," Grayson answered quickly, voice firm. "I'm on my way. Stay away from the windows. Call 911, wake up Rose, and turn on every light in the house. If it's the officer, we'll sort it out in a hurry."

"Okay, I'll do that now—" A muffled thud interrupted her, followed by a sudden shout from down the hall.

Aunt Rose!

"Oh, no!" She gasped, dropping her phone as she launched herself from the bed with a yell. "I'm coming, Aunt Rose!"

Heart in her throat, she ran toward the door, grabbing her mace from the dresser and rushing down the hall, the dogs at her heels. Flinging the guest room door open, she barged in, mace at the ready, prepared for the worst.

The window was wide open, screen missing. The curtains flapped in the breeze. Bright silver illuminated the room.

And a man. Dressed in dark clothing and wearing a ski mask.

He advanced toward Rose who was backing toward the wall, mace in hand. Ducking his head, the intruder shielded his face with one hand to avoid the foam mace shooting out from Rose's special-edition breast-cancer-awareness canister. The mace did actually have as good a range as the canister, and Rose, had claimed. Unfortunately, Rose's aim was not as reliable. From the amount of foam on the floor, wall, and intruder himself, there couldn't be much left in the canister.

The intruder must have known it. He snagged Rose's nightgown, jerked her toward him. Something glinted in his free hand.

Laney's pulse jumped. A gun.

Without thinking, she rushed toward them, bare feet slipping on the hardwood floor slick with foam mace. The dogs followed her in.

"Halt!" Laney commanded the dogs to keep them out of the mace. The dogs stopped immediately at the emergency command. Both Rose and the intruder looked her way.

Aunt Rose ineffectively pelted the man with her small fist and the mace can, her face flushed and angry. Foam mace covered the left side of the intruder's ski mask. Though his left eye was squinted shut, he glared at Laney with his unaffected right eye. It was then he caught sight of the dogs behind her and hesitated.

"Brody. Jax. Danger." On her command, the dogs growled. "Don't move, or you'll be dog food," she yelled, mace at the ready.

It was a bluff, a scare tactic. Jax and Brody were search dogs, and not cross-trained in protection. But their teeth were bared, their growls menacing. The man stilled. "Put your hands where I can see them and step away from my aunt." Laney's calm command belied her terror for Rose. Years spent working with dogs that were far more sensitive to moods than the average person had taught her to control her emotions.

The man released Rose, shoving her away from him and taking a step toward Laney, hands raised, gun still in his grasp. Glancing first at the door, then toward the window as if calculating his likelihood of a quick getaway, he took yet another step closer.

Could this be one of the kidnappers? If he was, Laney couldn't afford to let him get away. He could lead them to Olivia and the others. She needed to figure out how to detain him until help arrived.

"Drop the gun," she ordered, her gaze and the can of mace trained on him.

"That's not gonna happen," he sneered, teeth gleaming behind the ski mask as he stepped forward. Brody's growls turned to a menacing bark.

"Don't move another step," she warned him. "I mean it."

Behind him, Rose quietly sidled around the wall to the dresser. Grabbing a large vase of flowers and hoisting it over her head, she launched it with as much force as she could muster. Unfortunately she wasn't very strong, and the water-filled vase was heavy. It hit him near the base of the neck, covering him with flower petals and water as it deflected off his shoulder and smashed to the floor— shards of glass mixing with flowers, foam mace and water.

The man cursed, quickly turning on Rose. In a blink, she grabbed the empty mace canister and pitched it at the intruder. He deflected it easily, rushing toward her as she scrambled across the bed in an attempt to evade his reach.

She wasn't fast enough.

He grabbed Rose's ankle. She cried out, kicking him ineffectively with her other foot.

Not wanting to inadvertently spray Rose with the mace, Laney frantically scanned the room for something she could use as a weapon. Anything to give them a fighting chance until help arrived.

A lunge whip Laney used to evaluate play drive in puppies rested by the closet. Snatching it up, she furiously slashed at the man's head and hands with the heavy nylon cording. The last hit left a welt on the bare skin between his gloved hand and his sweatshirt sleeve, causing him to release his grip on Rose.

He angrily grabbed at the whip as it angled down toward his head, trying to yank it from Laney's grasp, but it was slick with foam mace.

Jerking it back, and ignoring biting shards of glass under her feet, Laney rushed toward the intruder. The only other weapon she had was the mace, so she brought the canister down with force on the side of his head and ear. Letting out a howl, he cursed again and came around swinging. Laney ducked. Scrambling backward, she narrowly avoided the blow. Her feet lost purchase on the slippery floor and flew out from under her. She landed on her backside, the jarring force sending pain shooting through her body all the way up to her aching head. She felt dizzy, sick, and then he was on her, one hand on her throat, the other pointing the gun. She lifted the mace, pointed and prayed.

Gravel crunched under the tires and pelted the bottom of Grayson's sedan as he sped along Laney's drive. It had been several minutes since Laney had called, and time wasn't on his side. It took only seconds for a life to be snuffed out. Grayson knew that all too well.

Pulling his car to an abrupt stop in the front drive, he noticed the officer in a heap by the open driver's-side door of the marked car—head bleeding, gun holster clearly empty. There was no time to check his condition.

Leaving his emergency lights flashing, Grayson rushed to the front door, the distant approach of another car on the gravel road giving him hope that backup was on the way.

The house was locked tight. He'd never be able to break down the solid oak door. Knowing that the sliding glass door to the kitchen was his best bet, he ran the length of the porch, vaulting over the railing and sprinting around the corner of the house.

"Laney! Rose!" he called out, racing toward an open window and the scuffling sounds of a struggle mixed with barks and growls.

"Gray! In here! Help!" Rose's voice.

Hoisting himself up, he dropped through the window, into the room.

Laney was on the floor, wrestling with a man for a gun. One of the dogs had a hold of the man's pant leg. The other dog was by Laney, barking and growling furiously. Rose was doing her best to help, pelting the intruder around the head and neck with a boot.

"Get back, Rose!" Grayson yelled, rushing forward as the man wrenched the gun from Laney's grasp and rose to his feet, turning the gun on her.

The quiet click of the trigger, then nothing.

No bullet. No blood.

And no way was Grayson giving the guy a second chance. He rammed into him. Hard. They were both thrown off-balance as Grayson grabbed for the guy's gun hand, twisting it around until the perp had no choice but to drop the gun. It clattered to the hardwood floor.

"Aunt Rose—get the lights!" Laney called out.

Balling his fist, Grayson slammed it into the guy's ribs, then quickly followed that blow with an uppercut to the jaw.

The lights flicked on, and Grayson dodged a punch. Then another. His opponent was slower, half-blinded by mace. But Grayson still had the image of Laney at the barrel end of the gun in his mind. Still heard the click of the trigger. He had no mercy as he returned the attempted blows with an onslaught of punches to the perp's face and ribs.

The guy dropped to his knees with a grunt.

Grayson helped him the rest of the way to the floor with a hard shove, then pressed his knee into the guy's back.

Reaching for his cuffs, he saw Laney going for the gun. "Leave it," he cautioned her.

Laney stopped short. Dressed in black yoga pants and a tank top, her feet were bare and bloody. Smudges of mace lined her bruise-covered jaw. Her hair fell in wild, tangled waves around her face. "What do we do now?" she asked, worrying her bottom lip. Somehow she managed to look both tough and vulnerable.

"There's a police cruiser pulling up to the house. You two meet the officers at the door and bring them back to me."

Ten minutes later, he and Laney were seated at the kitchen table while Rose busied herself making a pot of tea. Laney's foot was elevated. A paramedic used tweezers to extract small shards of glass. Grayson was certain it hurt, but probably not as much as being shot had. And she'd come close to having that happen again, close to dying.

She winced as a larger splinter of glass was removed.

"You holding up okay, Laney?" he asked, his eyes turning toward the suspect who'd been read his rights and brought to the kitchen to be cleaned up. His ski mask had been bagged as evidence, along with a glass-cutter and some duct tape. The only other thing he'd had on him was a folded piece of paper with Laney's address printed on it.

And the gun. He'd taken it from the patrol officer after he'd knocked the guy out.

"I'm great," she responded, and Grayson turned his full attention back to her. She had the greenest eyes he'd ever seen.

"You're lying," he replied with a soft smile.

"Maybe a little." She flinched as the paramedic dug another piece of glass from her foot.

One of the officers was none-too-gently wiping remnants of the mace from the intruder's face with a washcloth. Grayson wished he'd hurry. Having the guy who'd tried to kill Laney in the same room had to be disconcerting for her.

There was a flurry of sound from the foyer. Then Kent Andrews rushed into the kitchen with Deputy Chief Tom Wallace right behind him.

"What have we got?" Andrews asked Grayson. In his early fifties, Andrews was a fitness buff who made the gym part of his job. Grayson had brought him into the case six weeks ago when the first Maryland victim, an eight-year-old girl from Annapolis, had disappeared. Since then, Andrews kept an open line of communication between the MPD and Grayson. Though Grayson was used to working alone, he appreciated another set of eyes on the case file and ears on the streets.

"White male. Possibly late twenties, early thirties. No ID on him, and he won't give his name." Grayson sighed. "He's lawyered up, not talking."

"Typical."

Grayson nodded in agreement. "The officers are cleaning him up. Quite a bit of mace squeezed through openings of the ski mask he was wearing. We're hoping either Laney or Rose will recognize him."

"Any signs of an accomplice?" Wallace asked.

"Not that I could see. He appears to be working alone. How's the officer?"

"He's conscious. Paramedics are loading him into the ambulance," Andrews said. "He's a little fuzzy about what happened, but we surmise the suspect staged a distraction and attacked after the officer got out of the car to investigate, obviously stealing the gun while the officer was down."

"It was fortunate the safety was on and the perp didn't have a clue," Grayson replied.

Andrews nodded. "Right now we're canvassing the area to see if we can tie a vehicle to him. It stands to reason he either lives or is parked somewhere in the community and came up the gravel road."

"That's my thought, too," Grayson agreed. "Though there's still a slight possibility he has a car and driver waiting for him, or a scheduled pickup time with an accomplice."

"Agreed. This property backs right up to Route 2, I've got two cars searching," Andrews offered with a glance at the suspect, whose back was to them. "But the underbrush is heavy this time of the year, and he looks way too free of thorns, burrs or dirt to have taken that route."

"Sounds like you've got all the bases covered. I was going to see if I could call in some agents if you didn't have men to spare."

"This case is our number-one priority right now. We'll do what needs to be done." Grayson recognized the sincerity and determination in Andrews's tone.

"I know you will." Grayson cast a glance at Laney. "And by the way, this wasn't a random break-in. He had a piece of paper with Laney's address folded up in his pocket."

"He's as good as he's gonna get, Chief, but his eyes are still a little swollen shut." The officer grabbed the suspect by the arm, yanking him toward the kitchen table. Grayson took a good look at the suspect. The officer was right. The perp's eyes were red and irritated. The mace had done a job on him. The punch he'd taken to the face hadn't helped, either.

Grayson stood up, grabbing the suspect's other arm and turning him toward Laney. "Do you recognize him?"

Laney shook her head. Sighed.

"No." She bit her lip, resting her head in the palm of her hand. Grayson could see Laney was as disappointed as he was. If this had been one of the kidnappers, they would have been one step closer to finding Olivia and the other children. Instead, they had another mystery on their hands. Who was this guy, and how was he connected to the case?

"Rose, how about you?" Grayson asked. Rose came around from the kitchen counter, walked right up to the suspect and gave him a once-over.

"He doesn't look familiar." Rose took one step closer,

peering up at the suspect, and Grayson thought he felt the suspect twitch. "Nope. I've never seen him before."

"Get him out of here," Andrews said to the uniformed officers.

He then turned back toward Grayson. "What do you make of this, Agent?" Chief Andrews asked.

"It's got to be connected to Olivia's abduction."

Andrews nodded his agreement. "Can I speak with you in the foyer for a moment?" he asked.

Leaving Laney and Rose in the company of Deputy Chief Wallace, Grayson joined Chief Andrews in the foyer. "Here's what's bothering me about this. There have been a number of home invasions in the surrounding area lately. Same MO—a glass cutter and duct tape have been used to cut a pane of glass from a window so the robber can reach through to open the lock. We've kept the method out of the media."

Grayson hadn't been aware of that similarity. The implications were not good. He knew this break-in hadn't been random. If it had been, the perp would have aborted when he saw the uniformed officer outside. Besides, the slip of paper with Laney's name and address made it clear that she'd been specifically targeted. But someone obviously wanted the break-in to look like it was connected to the recent home invasions.

Someone with access to law enforcement files.

"I don't like this, Andrews."

"I know where you're going with this," Andrews said quietly, "and unfortunately, I'm thinking the same thing. There's a leak somewhere, and whoever it is has access to MPD files."

"Can you pull the files from the break-in cases? We can review them to see who might have had knowledge of the abduction and shooting tonight."

"Yeah, I'll do that, but I know every man in the precinct, and I can't think of one who would want Laney hurt."

Grayson knew Andrews wanted to believe that his men were honorable, but unfortunately, things were not always as they seemed. "You could be right. I'd also like to send a forensic expert down here to triage your computer networks. It's possible that your networks have been hacked—that you have a leak, but it's not from one of your own."

"Your forensics expert can have full access. I'll let our IT guy know he's to cooperate fully."

"Thanks. I'll have my laptop triaged, as well." Even though Grayson hoped the leak wasn't in his own house, the fact remained there *was* a leak—either in the local PD or the FBI—and he had to check out every possibility. He'd kept his suspicions to himself, sharing them only with his supervisor, Michael King, and his friend and mentor, retired FBI profiler Ethan Conrad. Like Grayson, both men were reluctant to believe the leak was in the FBI. But they'd agreed he had to look at all scenarios equally.

"Has anyone taken statements from Laney and Rose?" Andrews inquired.

"Not yet."

"I'll do that now."

"Can you step up patrol in the area until sunrise?" Grayson asked. "I'm going to stay here until then if Laney agrees. I've also asked Special Agent in Charge Michael King to authorize FBI protection starting tomorrow."

"There will be a car on this property until morning, Agent. With two officers," Andrews stated matter-of-factly, glancing into the kitchen, where Laney and Rose were quietly talking. "There's no way I'm leaving Laney's safety to chance."

"Then that makes two of us," Grayson said. And judging from the events of the night, he suspected that keeping Laney and her aunt safely out of trouble might be more of a challenge than Andrews thought.

EIGHT

An hour after the police carted the suspect away, Laney sipped a cup of now-cold tea and waited to be asked the same questions another fifty times. She was pretty sure that was how many times she'd already been asked them.

She wasn't annoyed by Kent's thorough interview. She was exhausted. She eyed the police chief as he paced across the room, pivoted and headed her way again.

"So," he continued, "what you're saying is that—"

"I've never seen the man before. I don't know why he broke into the house. I don't know what he wanted. Aside from the fact I tried to stop a kidnapping, I can't think of any reason why anyone would want to hurt me or my aunt."

Grayson snorted, and Laney was pretty sure he was trying to hold back a laugh.

He hadn't said much since the interview began, just leaned against the counter, nursing a cup of coffee and eyeing her intently.

She'd tried not to notice.

It had been difficult.

The guy exuded masculinity, confidence, kindness. All the things she'd have wanted in a man if she'd actually wanted a man in her life at all.

"Sorry to keep asking you the same questions, Laney,"

Kent said. "But sometimes things become clearer the more we go over them."

"I think this is all pretty clear," she responded, standing on legs that felt a little weak and walking to the sink. She washed her cup, set it in the drainer. She felt...done. With the questions, with the interview, with what seemed like an endless night.

She needed to sleep. She wanted to pull the curtains back from the window so she'd be awakened by the sun rising above the trees. Sunrise was always her favorite time of day. It reminded her of new beginnings, second chances.

"I think she's had enough," Grayson said quietly. No demands. No commands. But there was no doubt he was saying the interview was over.

She almost turned around and told him that she could take care of ending it herself, but she was too tired to protest. The past few years had been tough, digging out of the hole of mourning and guilt, rebuilding her life into something that resembled normal. It had worn her down. So had all the events of the past ten hours.

"I guess I have everything I need. You get some rest, Laney." Kent patted her shoulder, the gesture a little awkward and rough but strongly sincere.

"I will." She forced a smile and walked him to the door.

She thought Grayson would leave, too, but he just waited while she said goodbye to Kent, didn't even make a move toward the door as she waited with it open wide. The sky was dark, dawn's glow not yet peeking above the trees.

"You should probably go, too," she said, and he shook his head.

"I don't think so."

"What's that supposed to mean?"

"It means that he wants to help me with this crossword puzzle," Aunt Rose said as she looked up from the dining room table. "I'm stumped, and I've heard that FBI agents are very intelligent."

"I'm not sure that's true in my case," Grayson said with a smile. "But I'll be happy to help if I can."

Laney didn't have the energy to argue with either of them. Shutting the door, she retreated to the family room.

Not only was she exhausted, but her headache was returning, the dull throb making her stomach churn.

She dropped into her grandfather's chair and pulled one of the handmade quilts across her lap and shoulders. Grayson and Rose were discussing which five-letter word best fit Rose's puzzle, and she let her eyes close, let herself drift on the quietness of their voices, the gentle cadence of their conversation.

It felt…nice to have other people in the house. Paws clicked along the wood floor, and she opened her eyes to see Grayson crossing the foyer from the dining room into the family room, Jax and Brody at his heels. The dogs seemed to have taken a liking to the FBI agent.

"It's been quite a night," he commented as he sat on the couch across from her, the dogs taking their spots on the dog beds in the corner. "How are you holding up?"

"Pretty well, all things considered." She smiled.

"God was watching out for you and Rose tonight, Laney." Grayson ran a tanned hand through his hair.

Laney admired his conviction, but it was one she had a hard time sharing. She'd gone to Sunday school every Sunday as a child, had prayed every night for her mother to get better. To be stronger. To leave her father. And every day those prayers went unanswered. As she'd gotten older, she'd stopped praying and started acting. She'd had to rely on her own ingenuity and street smarts to protect them both from her father.

"We definitely got lucky," she agreed.

"I don't believe in luck. Everything happens for a reason. The good and the bad. All the events of our lives, big and small, shape us into who we are. Prepare us for our purpose." He fingered the scar over his brow absently, and Laney again wondered how he'd gotten it. It was definitely an old scar, its jagged ridges faded. It didn't detract from his good looks, but rather gave his face more strength of character. He looked real. Not like some politician, musician, or model. Like a man who would risk his life for what he believed in.

"I hope you're right," she said, because she wanted to believe the way he did. She wanted to think that everything she'd been through had brought her to the place she was supposed to be. That was hard, though, with the weight of guilt on her shoulders, the sorrow heavy in her heart.

"I'm going to bed." Rose announced, standing on threshold of the foyer and the dining room. "A good night's sleep is important to keep the mind sharp."

"Good night, Rose." Grayson remained seated on the couch.

"I need to get some sleep, too," Laney admitted with a yawn. She hoped he would pick up on her not-so-subtle hint as she headed toward the foyer to let him out. "I guess we'll see you in a few hours, then…"

"I'm not leaving." Grayson's voice was firm.

"I'm afraid I have only one spare room, and Rose is using it."

"I'll be fine on the couch. The sun will be up in a few hours, and I'd just as soon keep watch on the house until that happens."

"Well, I personally think that's a good idea," Rose interjected. "I'm a little too tired to take on another intruder tonight—plus my can of mace is depleted. I'll get the blankets and the extra pillows." Without waiting for Laney's response, Rose headed down the hall.

"Well, then, I guess it's settled," Laney agreed, not

wanting to admit, even to herself, that she felt better knowing Grayson would be down the hall. "If you'll excuse me,
I need to go grab the pillows from the top shelf before Aunt
Rose takes it upon herself to get on the stepladder—we
definitely don't need another trip to the emergency room
tonight."

Grayson woke with a start.

He was up and on his feet in seconds, the pile of blankets Rose had given him falling to the floor. No sign of
any danger, and the dogs weren't barking.

Something clanged in the kitchen. A pan or pot, maybe.

He thought it might be Rose, and he went to join her,
stopping short when he spotted Laney standing at the sink.
The early-morning sun cast gold and amber highlights
through her silky hair as she put on the coffee and popped
an English muffin into the toaster. Jax and Brody acknowl-
edged him with brief glances, then continued sitting patiently by the counter, watching Laney's every move.

"Good morning."

Though he spoke softly, Laney gasped and turned toward him, clearly startled.

"I'm sorry," he said. "I didn't mean to scare you."

"It's not your fault. I was lost in my thoughts. I guess
I'm a little on edge, that's all." She grabbed two dog bowls
and a bag of food from the pantry. "Would you like a muffin or some coffee? I've just put on a pot," she asked while
preparing the dogs' food.

"A cup of coffee would be great. And I'd like to grab a
quick shower later this morning if you don't mind."

"Of course. Fresh towels and soap are under the cabi-
net in the hall bathroom. Unfortunately, I don't have any
clean clothes that would fit you…"

"I keep spare clothes in a duffel in my car."

"Then you're all set. And feel free to help yourself to

anything you need from the visitor kit I keep in the bathroom. Sometimes clients will stay overnight when they drop their dogs off, and I like to be prepared."

"That's not a surprise."

"What's that supposed to mean?"

"Just that you seem like the kind of person who prefers to have a plan in place."

"This from the guy that keeps spare clothes in a duffel in his car?" she retorted, placing the dogs' bowls down by the sliding glass door. Neither dog moved from its spot. Eyes trained on Laney, they watched as she crossed the room to the coffeepot and grabbed two mugs from the cupboard.

She glanced at the dogs. "Break," she commanded, and both went for their food.

"They're really well-behaved," he commented.

"Dogs need to understand their boundaries and limitations. Consistency in reinforcing those things is the key." She poured coffee into the mugs. "Milk or sugar?"

"Black is fine."

She leaned against the counter, sipping her coffee. Dressed in beige tactical pants, work boots and a white, long-sleeved T-shirt with the Wagging Tails Boarding and Training logo on it, it was clear she was ready to work. "Heading out to take care of the dogs?"

"It's what I do."

"Not without an escort."

"You're welcome to come along, but I've got some training to do, so I may be a while."

"How long have you been a dog trainer?"

"Professionally, since I was about nineteen—it helped pay my college living expenses—but I've been training dogs since I was eleven. I picked it up from my grandfather. He's the one who started this training facility. He mostly trained police dogs for protection work and drug sniffing back then. Some of my best childhood moments were spent in the kennels with the dogs." Her smile lit her eyes. "But then, what kid wouldn't like playing with dogs all day?"

She pulled her hair up in a ponytail, tying it off with an elastic band she'd worn around her wrist. She wore no makeup, the bruise at her jawline now a bluish green; the end of the red, jagged bullet wound and one staple were clearly visible at her temple near her hairline, but none of it detracted from her quiet beauty. She had an inner strength and calmness about her that he was sure was part of her success as a dog trainer. Grayson had always believed dogs to be perceptive about people's character and moods.

"I've got to head out. My staff will be here by eight to help open the kennels, and I have a potential new client coming at nine for a puppy evaluation—it should be interesting because I've never worked with a Leonberger before. Her name is Maxine."

Grayson had never even *heard* of a Leonberger. "Do we have time for me to grab my laptop? I've got some case files I want to go over."

"Can you do it in two minutes?"

"It's out in my car. I can do it sixty seconds."

"Challenge on," she responded, lifting her wrist and staring at her watch.

He made it back with the laptop in fifty seconds, because he was pretty sure she wouldn't wait the entire sixty.

She was still in the kitchen, the sunlight still playing in her hair.

He thought he'd like to see her outdoors, working with her dogs, doing what she did best.

And that wasn't a good thought to be having about his key witness.

"So what are you planning to tell your staff about your injuries?" he asked, because he needed to get his mind back on protecting Laney. Even though it seemed certain her connection to the case had been leaked, he still thought it wise to downplay her involvement, to keep the reason for her injuries quiet.

"I think explaining your presence, and that of the patrol car, could be just as difficult, actually. What would you suggest?"

"For now, let's blame your injuries and police protection on the break-in and call me an old friend."

"We can try it, but I'm not good at subterfuge. If they start asking questions, that story will fall apart quickly."

"Well, I guess you'll have to keep them too busy to ask questions."

"That part probably won't be much of a problem." She opened the sliding glass door, letting the dogs out into the yard.

Grayson followed Laney to the kennels, where she busied herself filling water bowls with a two-gallon jug. She had released most of the dogs, about fifteen in all, into a fenced enclosure in the center of the kennel that appeared to be an indoor training area. The morning quiet was now broken with lots of barking, yapping, jumping and running around. He noticed one dog, a large Rottweiler, remained in its enclosure. "What's wrong with that one?" he asked out of curiosity.

"He's here as a board-and-train. He's a rescue, but he's dog-aggressive and hard to control on walks. He's improved since he's been here, but I don't trust him to play unsupervised yet."

"That's too bad."

"He's young, and he's smart. His new owners love him. He'll have a happy ending." She smiled.

A door opened at the back of the facility. A girl, about fifteen, came out, hands filled with two buckets overflowing with metal dog bowls. An older teen boy was behind her, pushing a cart piled high with dog food.

"Guys, I'd like you to meet Grayson DeMarco. He's an old friend. Grayson, this is Riley Strong and Bria Hopewell, my staff."

Riley stepped out from behind the cart, extending a hand to Grayson. "Nice to meet you," he said, pumping Grayson's hand just a little harder than socially acceptable. Not at all threatened by Riley's obvious territorial gesture, Grayson smiled.

"The pleasure's mine," he countered, returning the handshake. He had no doubt Riley knew he was no match physically for Grayson, but he appreciated the kid's protective posture and wondered if Laney recognized his obvious devotion to her.

Bria stepped forward, pushing her glasses up on her nose and extending her hand, as well. She was taller than Laney, about five-six, and way too skinny. Her natural blond hair was pulled up into a ponytail, the bangs falling into her eyes. She barely met Grayson's eyes as she mumbled, "Nice to meet you," before dropping his hand like a hot potato. Grayson had seen kids act like that before, and usually for a reason other than severe shyness. He made a mental note to ask Laney about Bria's story later.

"What's up with the cop car outside?" Riley asked.

"We had a break-in last night, and Chief Andrews thought it would be safer to leave some officers here." A red flush crept into Laney's cheeks. She was right. She was possibly the worst liar Grayson had ever seen. The kids didn't seem too perceptive, however, accepting her explanation and going about their task of feeding the dogs.

"You're welcome to use my office if you need a place to work, Grayson. Here, let me show you where it is."

"This is a nice setup," he commented, following her through the facility.

"I renovated when I took over the business from Granddad about two years ago."

Grayson noticed a sprinkler system in the ceiling, and cameras in the corners focused on the training ring.

"You have security cameras in your kennels but won't get an alarm in your house?" Grayson asked. It seemed to him that her money would have been better spent equally on the house and the kennel.

"The cameras are for recording training sessions only. They're not set up for around-the-clock monitoring."

Grayson's phone vibrated on his hip. "Mind if I take this?"

"Why would I? You've got work to do, and so do I. My office is this way." She led him past the reception area, down a small corridor that ended at an office and storage area as Grayson answered the phone.

"DeMarco."

"Andrews here. The arson investigator is wrapping things up. He'll have the official report to us this afternoon, but the fuse at the hospital was deliberately blown. He confirmed his initial assessment of arson."

Just as Grayson had expected. "What about the surveillance video?"

"No one was in or around that area except the security guard. I've sent a patrol car out to his house to bring him to the precinct for further questioning," Andrews said.

"Good. We need to press him. Any ID yet on our perp from the break-in?" he asked, meeting Laney's eyes. She looked worried. She should be. It was obvious the kidnappers knew she had survived. There was no doubt the blown fuse, the intruder, all of it were connected with the intent of finding and silencing her.

"Prints were a match for Stephen Fowler," Andrews continued. "Two-time loser. Just released nine months ago after serving a four-year stretch for B&E. His car was parked at his parents' house in the neighborhood, but they claimed they'd not seen him since his release. Father seemed pretty angry over a stolen family car a few years back—claims he'd cut off all ties. Mom may be maintaining contact without telling dad, but I don't think either had any knowledge of his actions last night."

"Fowler say anything useful?"

"No. He's still clammed up. It doesn't look like he'll be able to make bail. Maybe another night in jail will loosen his tongue."

"Maybe. We could definitely use a break. Right now I'm pinning all my hopes on Laney being able to ID a suspect," Grayson said.

"Do you think we should reconsider moving her to a safe house?" Andrews asked.

"The problem is, I don't know who to trust. I'd feel better if she was here, with a combination of police and FBI protection for the next few days."

"I'll support that. I'll rotate officers out front," Andrews said. "Any word on the FBI protection detail?"

"Best case scenario, tonight or tomorrow. I'll stay around until we get more people lined up."

"I'll be by in a few hours to drop Murphy off. You can let me know then if you think we need to take additional precautions."

Grayson checked his watch. "Actually, I've got the sketch artist flying in soon. If you're going to be here, I'll feel better about leaving Laney to pick the sketch artist up from the airport. My plan is to bring her directly here—the quicker we get the sketches done, the better."

"That won't be a problem," Andrews said. "You still planning to bring in that computer-forensics guy? Because if you're not, I'm calling someone in. If there's a leak in my department, I want to know it."

"She's coming, but she's not a guy. I called in a favor and got the leading cyber-forensics investigator in the country." He didn't mention that Arden was his sister. No need for that. Andrews would figure it out soon enough.

"She's FBI, too?"

"No. She's brains for hire. An independent contractor. But I know I can trust her, and that's all that matters right now."

Grayson said a quick goodbye and disconnected.

"Well?" Laney demanded, her eyes deeply shadowed, the bruise on her jaw purple and green against her pale skin.

"I think you heard most of it. The arson team confirmed that the fuse box had been tampered with, and the perp from the break-in is still not talking. Kent's planning to bring Murphy..."

A sudden commotion in the kennels, followed by a reverberating crash and a piercing scream, had Grayson on high alert, hurrying toward the office door. "Wait here," he ordered Laney as he rushed into the kennels, pulling the door shut behind him.

Drawing his gun, he raced to the indoor training ring, scanning the facility for the source of danger.

He didn't have to look far.

Near the entry of the indoor training facility, a brown-and-black mass of fur on legs was excitedly pulling on its leash. It must have weighed a good seventy or eighty pounds. The poor owner was putting all his strength into holding it at bay as it wagged its tail excitedly and tried to reach Riley and the food cart. It had already managed to barrel over Bria, knocking her off her feet and scattering metal dog bowls all over the concrete floor. Riley was trying to pull her up, one eye warily trained on the furry menace.

Unexpectedly, the pup pulled free, launching himself in a ball of unbridled excitement toward the teens and the food cart. Grayson cringed, but it was like watching a train wreck about to happen. He just couldn't look away.

Footsteps pounded on the ground behind him, and he whirled around, ready for danger. Laney was there, wild auburn curls flying around her face, eyes wide with surprise. She held a long metal pole, her knuckles white from her grip on it.

"I guess," she said, as he turned back and saw the furry beast had its head in a bucket of dog food, "that is Maxine."

NINE

Maxine was a darling, but she was a wild one.

Laney barely managed to get her back into her owners' SUV after the evaluation was done.

They drove away, waving wildly, probably in gratitude that Maxine hadn't killed Bria or Riley.

Maxine stuck her head out the side window, her tongue lolling out.

"I can't believe that thing is only five months old." Grayson commented.

"She's cute, isn't she?" Laney asked.

"Cute? I don't think anything that big can be called cute."

"Beauty is in the eye of the beholder," she responded absently, turning to clean up the mess left in Maxine's wake.

"You shouldn't have come running out of the office. You know that, right?" Grayson asked, helping right the cart and scoop what was left of the food back onto it.

"What was I supposed to do? Cower in my office, hoping and praying that the screams weren't my staff members being slaughtered?"

"You thought they were being slaughtered, and you came outside with this?" He lifted her grandfather's old catching pole, a tool used to control vicious, potentially dangerous dogs. It was a five-foot-long aluminum rod with a grip on one end and a retractable noose on the other.

She had never used one herself, and in all the years she had worked with her grandfather, she had never seen him use one, either. But when she'd prepared to leave the office to find the source of the screaming, it had been the only potential weapon within her reach.

"It made sense at the time." She shrugged, her hair sliding along her neck and falling away from the wound on her head. She'd almost died trying to save a stranger. It shouldn't surprise him that she'd come running to rescue her employees.

"It would have made more sense to stay where I left you. I have a gun, Laney, and I'm trained to take down criminals."

"And I'm trained to take care of the people who work for me. I'm not going to sit back and let them be hurt because I'm too afraid to act." Her voice shook—she hoped he didn't notice.

"Okay," he said, sounding less like he truly agreed and more like he simply didn't want to argue with her.

"What's that supposed to mean?" she asked, her voice laced with suspicion.

"It means you're exhausted. And you need some rest."

"I need to meet with that sketch artist."

"She'll be here this afternoon."

"But will that be soon enough? The kidnappers know I'm alive. They may move Olivia and the other children sooner rather than later."

"Moving them early would take a lot of coordination and effort," he reminded her, but she heard the doubt in his voice. She knew he'd hoped to lull the kidnappers into a false sense of security by making them believe she was dead. Since that plan had fallen through, he had to be just as worried as she was that the abductors would decide to cut their losses and leave the area with the children they'd already taken.

"That doesn't mean they won't do it, and once the kids are out of the country, they may never be found."

"I suspect they have a quota of children to meet, and the kidnappers are not going to jeopardize their payday just yet. Not until they've exhausted all other options."

"As in tried everything to get rid of me?"

"Something like that. Come on. Let's go back to the house. You're looking a little pale."

She had a feeling he was being diplomatic. If the aching exhaustion she felt was any indication, she probably looked like five miles of rough road. "I'm feeling a little pale, too, but I have dogs to take care of."

"Your staff can handle it." He pressed his hand to her lower back, urging her to the house.

He looked even more worried when she didn't bother to protest.

They walked to the house silently, her steps slow and a little unsteady. The adrenaline that had shot through her when she'd heard the screams of her staff was fading, leaving her drained and hollow. When she'd heard Bria and Riley calling out, her heart sunk with the certainty that she had—once again—put the people who trusted her in harm's way. Now her mind was filled with dark memories and all she wanted was to crawl into bed and hope that sleep would push those memories away, at least for a little while.

"You know what?" she murmured without looking at him. "I think I'm going to lie down for a while."

She didn't give him a chance to say he thought it was a good idea. She just walked down the hall and into her bedroom, closing the door behind her.

Sunlight tracked along the ceiling, the house filled with noises. Rose's voice. Grayson's. The television blasting *The Price Is Right*. Dishes clanked, and the sweet smell of fresh baked treats filled the room. The dogs sniffed at the closed bedroom door. She could hear their quiet snuffling breaths, but she was too tired to let them in. She allowed herself to drift in that sweet place between waking and sleeping, that soft spot where memories didn't intrude and circumstances didn't matter so much.

Someone knocked on the door. "Laney," Rose called. "Do you want some tea?"

It was Rose's cure-all, and most times Laney would humor her aunt by having a cup. This wasn't most days, and she kept her eyes closed, pretending to be asleep as the door swung open.

"Laney, dear?" Rose whispered. The floorboards creaked as she approached the bed, and Laney caught a whiff of her aunt's lavender body wash. "Are you awake?"

"I'm trying really hard not to be," Laney muttered.

"Oh. Well, then, I'll just leave you to it. That good-looking FBI agent is sitting in the living room having one of my famous cinnamon rolls. I thought you might like one, too."

"First of all," Laney said, finally opening her eyes, "you know his name is Grayson. Second, your famous cinnamon rolls come from a can, so I'm not sure how you can even call them yours or famous."

"They *are* famous, Laney. The commercials for them are all over the television. I made them. Therefore, they are mine," Rose huffed.

"I'm sure several million other people have also made them." Laney sat up, her entire body achy and old-feeling. "You didn't just come in here to ask me if I wanted a cinnamon roll. What's up?"

"I'm worried about you," Rose admitted, sitting on the edge of the bed and placing a hand on Laney's thigh. "Since when do you lie around in the middle of the day?"

"Since I got shot in the head?"

"Don't try to be funny, Laney. This isn't the time for it."

"Really, Aunt Rose. You don't need to worry. I'm fine."

"The bruise on your jaw and the staples in your scalp would say differently."

"What they say, Aunt Rose, is that I survived. That's a great thing. Not something to make you worry."

"I always worry about you, dear. Ever since that unfortunate incident—"

"I think I *will* have one of those cinnamon rolls." Laney stood so abruptly, her head swam.

"You can't keep running away from it forever, Laney." Rose grabbed her arm, her grip surprisingly strong for a woman of her age. "Eventually, you're going to have to do the hard work of letting go."

"I have let go." She just hadn't forgotten, would never forget.

"Then maybe what you really need is to grab on to something worth believing in." Rose planted her fists firmly on hips that sported bright pink running pants.

"I suppose you're going to tell me what that is?"

"*I* suppose that *you're* intelligent enough to figure it out yourself! But maybe not, since you've spent the past few years hiding in your safe little house, ignoring God's calling for your life!" She flung the last over her shoulder as she huffed out of the room.

Laney sank onto the bed, her muscles so tense she thought they might snap. She didn't like to talk about what had happened in Colorado. She didn't like to think about it. Of course, she still thought about it almost every day. How could she not? She'd lost three well-trained team members. Not just team members. Friends. All of them gone in a blink of an eye and the wild heaving of an avalanche. She rubbed the back of her neck, tried to force the memories away.

They wouldn't leave her. Despite what she'd said to Rose, she hadn't let go. She *couldn't* let go. She'd been responsible for her team, and she'd failed them.

There was nothing that could change that, nothing that could bring back the lives that had been lost.

Not even giving up search and rescue, a quiet voice inside reminded her.

She ignored it. She'd made the decision to retire Jax. It had been the right one to make. She was doing good things with her business, and she didn't see how that could be construed as ignoring God's calling.

Whatever that calling might be.

She frowned, eyeing the old family Bible that sat on her dresser. It had belonged to her grandfather, and he'd given it to her a few weeks before his death. She had opened it once, to read verses from it during his funeral. She touched the cover. Ran her fingers over the embossed letters that read *Travis Family Bible*. It was smooth as silk, decades of being handled and read leaving the old leather soft. She'd believed in God for as long as she could remember. What she hadn't believed was that He cared, that He had a purpose and a plan for her life.

Aunt Rose, though, was convinced otherwise.

So, apparently, was Grayson.

Laney wanted to believe it. She wanted to know everything that had happened would eventually lead her to the place she was supposed to be.

"Everything okay in here?" Grayson asked from the open doorway. He'd showered and changed into a clean set of black tactical pants and a black T-shirt with the FBI logo. Her breath caught as he smiled. He looked good. Great, even. And she'd have to be blind not to notice it.

"Yes."

"Then why did Rose stomp into the kitchen muttering something about stubborn nieces? You're not planning your escape, are you?"

"Not hardly." She laughed, her hand falling away from the Bible, the soft feel of its cover still on her fingers and in her mind. "She's just annoyed with me."

"Why?" He walked into the room, and it felt smaller, more intimate.

"Because I retired from search and rescue," she admitted, sidling past him and moving into the hall. The last thing she wanted was Grayson DeMarco in her bedroom.

"I read about that," he responded.

She stopped short, turning to face him. The hall was narrow, and they were close. She could see the stubble on his chin, the dark ring around his striking blue irises. "Where?"

"A local paper did a story about you a couple of years ago, remember?"

"Yes, but I didn't think anyone else did."

"I did a little research while you were resting and found it. I told you I planned to work this morning."

"I'm not sure I like that you were digging into my past. As a matter of fact, I'm pretty positive that I don't like it at all."

"I wasn't digging. I was doing background checks on everyone involved in the case."

"You need a background check on a witness?"

"Not every witness is an innocent bystander, Laney," he responded, eyeing her. "Now that I'm thinking about it, Rose was also muttering something about grumpy nieces."

"I am not grumpy!" Laney protested, even though she probably was.

"Sure you are. Sleep deprivation will do that to a person. Come on." He took her arm, his strong fingers curving around her biceps, their warmth seeping through her cotton shirt. "A little sugar will perk you right up."

"I don't need—"

"What you need," he cut her off, his expression serious, "is to let go and let someone take care of you for a while." He began leading her to the kitchen.

It was the second time in just a few minutes that someone had told her she needed to let go.

Maybe it was time, she thought, but she wasn't sure she knew how.

TEN

The cinnamon roll was surprisingly good, despite the slightly burnt edges. The conversation was better.

Grayson was funny and intelligent, and Laney would have been lying if she said she hadn't enjoyed spending time with him. But Grayson's easy banter couldn't belie his concern. He was reluctant to leave, even after Kent arrived with Murphy, who'd greeted Laney like a long-lost friend before eying Grayson suspiciously until introductions were made. Grayson had finally given her a stern reminder to stay in the house and left for the airport.

With Grayson gone, Laney tried not to watch the clock, counting the minutes until he'd return with the sketch artist. The armed officers in Laney's drive, plus the curtains pulled tightly closed throughout the house, were blatant reminders of the danger she was in. If that wasn't enough, the nagging headache and various aches and pains she had would have been.

She watched as Rose popped opened another container of cinnamon rolls. Despite her cheerfulness, she looked tired, her skin a little pale, her hair a little less bouncy than usual.

"Why don't you let me do that, Aunt Rose?" she asked, and Rose scowled.

"You think I'm too old to handle this?"

"I think that if I'm tired, you must be, too."

"Well, I am, but Grayson would probably enjoy a few more piping hot cinnamon rolls when he comes back, and you've never been all that good of a cook."

"This isn't cooking," Laney said, taking the can from her aunt's hands. "And you know that Grayson has only been gone forty minutes. If we bake these now, they won't be hot when he gets back."

"Truth be told," Rose admitted, "I want one. I stress-eat, dear. That's how I got these." She patted her hips, and Laney laughed.

"You've got nothing. Now, sit down. I'll take care of the rolls."

She helped her aunt to the chair, anxious to get her off her feet. The woman had more energy than most twenty-year-olds, but she wasn't twenty, and she could easily overdo it.

Once Rose had settled into the chair, Laney opened the container, peeled out the rolls and placed them in the baking dish. After sticking them in the oven, she did a half dozen other things that were everyday and easy. All the while, her heart slammed against her ribs. Her throat was dry. Every minute, she expected something to scratch against the kitchen window, someone to kick in the kitchen door.

Sure, they had armed police officers outside, but that hadn't made any difference the previous night.

As if thinking about it made it happen, the back door flew open.

She screamed, the sound choking off as she saw a police officer standing in the doorway.

"Sorry about that, ma'am," he said, his gaze shooting to a spot just past her shoulder. She glanced back and saw Kent on the kitchen threshold.

"What's going on?" he asked, his tone cold, his eyes icy.

Maybe he thought the police officer was a threat. Whatever the case, the young officer swallowed hard, took a
step backward.

"Mills Corner store and gas station has just been held up
at gunpoint. Dispatch has called us in since we're the closest officers. You cool with us going to the scene, Chief?"

Kent hesitated, then nodded. "Go ahead. Call in to dispatch to have a couple of officers head out here to fill in,
though. We don't want to take any chances."

"Will do!" He raced back outside. Seconds later, the
sound of a siren blasted through the afternoon stillness.

"I don't like this," Kent said with a scowl, pacing to the
front window and pulling back the curtain. Murphy, sensing his anxiety, was instantly at his side. "That gas station is so far off the beaten track, it's nearly impossible to
find if you don't know where to look. It's too much of a
coincidence that it just happened to be robbed today. Call
those kids back from the kennel, Laney. I'm going to take
Murphy with me and do a sweep of the property. Make
sure everything looks clear. Let the kids in, lock the door
and stay inside."

He snapped a lead on Murphy, issued a command and
opened the sliding glass door.

As soon as he disappeared from view, Laney texted
Bria and Riley, telling them to come to the house. The
chief was right. The little gas station had been around for
as long as Laney could remember, and as far as she could
recall, it had never been robbed before. The mom-and-pop
store offering cheap prices on junk food and milk didn't
look like much. It certainly didn't look like much money
could be found there.

Riley knocked on the sliding glass door, and Laney
opened it, waving the teen inside. Bria was right behind
him, her eyes wide. "What's going on?" she asked. "More
trouble?"

"Not yet," Laney responded, keeping her tone calm. She didn't want to scare her employees.

"Meaning you're expecting trouble?" Riley asked. "Because if you are, I want to go home and get my hunting rifle."

'There's no need for that," she cut him off. "We're not even sure there's actually any trouble."

"Then Bria and I should go back to the kennel. We've got a lot of work to do." He opened the slider, stepping outside. One of the kenneled dogs barked, the frantic sound a warning that Laney recognized immediately. Trouble. Danger.

She met Riley's eyes. "Was everything okay when you left?"

"It was fine," he responded. "We were…" His voice trailed off as a wisp of gray smoke spiraled up from the corner of the kennel.

The scent of it followed, wafting into the kitchen, stinging Laney's nostrils.

"Fire!" she shouted. "Rose, call 911! There's a fire at the kennel."

Rose grabbed the kitchen phone while Laney raced out the sliding glass doors toward the kennel, Riley and Bria close behind. They needed to get the dogs out first and then worry about containing the damage to the kennels.

"You guys get the hose and meet me by the outdoor dog runs. We're about to put the emergency evacuation system to the test. Remember, under no circumstances do either of you go into the facility." Her mind racing, Laney knew she could be walking into a trap. As much as she wanted to get the dogs out safely, she could not endanger either Riley or Bria to do it.

Laney was at the kennel entrance in moments. She'd had an emergency release switch designed to open all the dog runs at once. She'd tested it after it was installed but had never needed to use it again.

Throwing the facility door open, she rushed in. Smoke billowed from under her office door. So far the flames were contained behind it. Laney knew the sprinkler heads would activate only with direct heat. There were two sprinkler heads in her office. She hoped they would contain the fire. She pulled open the dog run control panel and yanked down the emergency release lever. The grinding sound of the gates opening was an immediate relief. Now it was just a matter of getting into each run, putting a leash on the dogs and taking them to the outside training pavilion until help arrived.

A shadow passed across the open door.

Was someone there? "Kent?" she yelled, hoping the chief had finally arrived. The property was large, but there was no way he'd missed the thick cloud of smoke that was engulfing the area.

"It's Riley," the teen responded. "I thought you could use an extra set of hands."

"I told you not to come in the kennel," she snapped as Riley appeared at the threshold. She didn't want him to become an unintended target.

A sudden movement behind Riley caught her eye.

A man ran toward the entrance to the kennels, a baseball cap pulled low over his face, a tire iron in his hand.

"Riley! Look out!" Laney warned, rushing toward him. Riley turned, ducking and bringing his arm up in an attempt to block the blow from the tire iron. Though his arm took the brunt of the blow, the tire iron still caught him on the side of the head. He crumpled to the ground in a heap.

"No!" Laney cried out as the man roughly nudged Riley with his foot, stepping callously over the body of the unconscious teenager.

She couldn't see the man's face, but something about

him was eerily familiar. He had the same wiry frame and runner's build as the gun-wielding kidnapper. A familiar fear ran up Laney's spine as he advanced toward her, tire iron poised for attack.

Glancing around, she saw the catching pole resting against the front desk where she had left it that morning. Wielding it like a sword, she swung it at him. He dodged back to avoid the blow. She swung again, the tip of the pole hitting his hand.

"You're going to pay for that!" he growled.

He lunged forward, the tire iron arcing toward her head.

She ducked, swung the pole again. He grabbed the end and tried to rip it from her hands.

"Laney! Where are you?" Kent called from the other side of the kennels.

"Here, Kent! Quick! Help!"

At the sound of Kent's voice, the man dropped the catching pole and darted toward her. The tire iron whizzed through the air.

She felt it glance off her arm as she ran toward Kent's voice.

She thought she'd feel it again, slamming into the back of her skull or the side of her head. She was sure that at any moment, the man would be on her.

Instead, she felt nothing. Heard nothing. She glanced over her shoulder and saw him disappearing into the woods.

She was safe.

But she didn't feel safe.

She felt terrified.

Kent called out again, and she managed to respond, her heart in her throat as she turned back and knelt beside Riley. He groaned, his eyes fluttering open. He was alive. She was thankful for that. She had to keep him that way. Keep Rose and Bria safe.

A task that seemed to grow more difficult by the hour. If something happened to any of them, she'd never forgive herself. She was all too familiar with that scenario. Her failure to protect them would haunt her dreams. And her waking hours.

A fire truck, an ambulance, two police cruisers and a K-9 unit were still in the yard when Grayson navigated the gravel road. Andrews had called and briefed him on the attack and Grayson's mind was racing as he parked quickly, jumping out of his sedan and opening the passenger door for the sketch artist.

"Slow down," Willow Scott demanded, her curly blond hair pulled into a loose bun, the hairstyle matching her no-nonsense business suit perfectly. "Rushing isn't going to change what's already happened," she said, her long stride easily keeping up with his as he jogged toward the house.

"Moving slow isn't going to keep more from happening," he growled, frustrated with himself, with Kent, with the two officers who'd left their post to respond to the falsified report of an armed robbery.

The door flew open as he jogged up the porch stairs, and Kent Andrews appeared, a streak of soot on his cheek and a scowl deepening the lines in his face. "This the sketch artist?" he asked, gesturing to Willow.

"I am," Willow responded, moving past him and into the house, adjusting a bag of art supplies she had slung over her shoulder. "Where's the witness?"

"In the kitchen. She thinks the guy who was out here today might be one of the kidnappers from last night."

"How'd he get away?" Grayson asked.

"I'm pretty sure he had an accomplice parked out on the highway. Murphy and I scoured the woods. No sign of anyone, though Laney clearly saw him disappear into the trees."

"That's unfortunate. I really want to ID these guys quickly," Grayson responded.

"Well, if Laney is as good a witness as you think she will be, we'll be able to run a sketch through the system before the day is out," Willow interjected. "If the partial prints or DNA profile from the gun recovered at the scene pan out, your case will be airtight—and if either of the kidnappers is in the system, we'll have a positive ID in no time."

Grayson was banking on it. The FBI's new facial recognition program was able to compare surveillance images and even sketches against the FBI's national database of mug shots in minutes. That's why he'd brought Willow in. She'd had a hand in developing the system and the highest hit ratio of any artist using it. "Let's hope both perps have criminal records."

"There's a good probability they do. You don't get involved in this type of crime overnight. I'm betting these guys are career criminals."

"Let's get this done, then." Grayson said, leading the way to the kitchen.

The house bustled with activity. Firefighters, police and ambulance personnel were all milling around, eating freshly baked chocolate chip cookies that Rose was passing around on a platter. Despite the cookies, the air was still ripe with the scent of smoke, the sliding glass door open, cool air tinged with a hint of moisture drifted in.

He scanned the room and found Laney seated in a chair at the table. She caught his eye and smiled. She looked young, her hair scraped into a ponytail, her eyes shadowed. "You made it back," she said.

"Better late than never, I guess." He took a seat beside her, the acrid stench of smoke heavier there. Though her clothes were smudged with soot, her face and hands looked freshly scrubbed.

"You're not late," Rose cut in. "You're just in time for a cookie." She handed him one, and Grayson ate it.

It tasted like dust. Or maybe mud.

"Good?" she asked, beaming as she held out the platter. "Have another."

"Thanks, but we've got a lot of work to do. Maybe you could—"

"Say no more!" she interrupted. "Bria and I will check on the dogs, but we'll go see Riley first. He's conscious but the paramedics want him assessed at the hospital. His parents just arrived and they're planning to head over there with him. Bria, grab that platter of cookies in case anyone needs a snack."

Seconds later, Kent had cleared the rest of the room, then joined firefighters and police outside. Willow took a seat on the opposite side of Laney, smiling as she introduced herself. She was good at what she did. Great at it, and part of that gift was in her ability to make the witness feel comfortable and confident.

She emptied her bag of supplies onto the kitchen table.

Grayson had seen her in action before, but he pulled up a chair and watched, anyway. He needed this sketch to match something in the database. Despite the police presence, he was worried. Laney had been attacked again. Both times she'd been under the protection of the MPD. Both times, he was not around.

Had the attacker known Grayson would be at the airport picking up the sketch artist? The timing of the fire seemed to indicate that, but only a few people had known when Willow would arrive.

Was the leak in the FBI or in the local PD? It was a question Grayson needed answered. Until then, he'd be taking extra precautions. And unless it was absolutely necessary, he wouldn't be leaving Laney's side.

He'd confirmed the FBI protection detail had been processed and should arrive before the day was out. It couldn't come quickly enough for Grayson.

His phone vibrated, and he glanced at his caller ID. Ethan Conrad.

Good. Grayson needed to run a few things by him.

Though retired, Ethan remained an influential and well-connected force in the FBI. He had lobbied for Grayson to be assigned the kidnapping ring case when the Boston field agent stepped down. He'd been Grayson's sounding board during the past few months, helping him weed through and make sense of dozens of reports and reams of information from field offices in California and Boston.

Grayson didn't bother excusing himself, didn't want to interrupt the flow of Willow's work. Instead, he stepped out the sliding glass door. "Grayson here. What's up?"

"Just making sure Willow arrived as scheduled. I spoke with Michael this afternoon, and he's antsy to get a sketch of the perps into the system."

"Same here," Grayson responded. "Willow's working with Laney Kensington now. The sooner we can identify our suspects, the better. There've been additional attempts on Laney's life."

"I thought you requested twenty-four-hour protection."

"I did. MPD's been covering so far and FBI is on the way. But our perps seem to know my schedule, and they use it to their advantage." He explained briefly, and Ethan sighed.

"Your theory seems accurate, then. We've got a leak. In the bureau or in the police precinct."

"I'm inclined to think it's in our office. Who else would have known what time Willow would arrive?"

"Anyone with access to airport databases can search for a name and find out when that person's flying in or out of a city. Willow is one of the most sought-after sketch artists in the country, and this kidnapping ring is savvy enough to pinpoint who you'd likely bring in and follow that person's activities. It would be easy enough to figure out what time she'd be arriving."

He was right, but Grayson couldn't shake the feeling that the leak was somewhere in the FBI's house. "I've got Arden coming in to take a look at the computer system at the local police department. If any information is being filtered out or in there, we'll know it."

"You've got that right." Ethan chuckled. "She won't miss anything."

"Do you have time to look through some case files for me, see if there's something I missed?" Grayson asked.

"Send the files to me over the FTP site. I'll grab them from the server and start reading through them tonight."

"Thanks. And Ethan, let's keep our suspicions quiet. If the leak *is* a federal agent, we don't want to give him a chance to cover his tracks."

"You know me better than that. I'll call if anything jumps out at me from the files. In the meantime, stay focused. This kidnapping ring has got to be stopped before any more families are destroyed."

Disconnecting from the call, Grayson paced the length of the back deck. He didn't want to believe the leak could be one of their own. But he couldn't afford to bury his head in the sand. *Someone* was leaking information to the kidnappers. There might be a computer hacker accessing the online systems, but the information the perps had went deeper than that. They seemed to know who would be where, and when. There was no way for them to know so much without an informant.

Worse, Grayson was beginning to believe the head of the child trafficking ring might be hiding behind an FBI badge. The cases spanned three states and international waters. It was possible someone in the state PD was on the payroll, but there was no way that person was the mastermind. It had to be a nationally connected source, and the FBI was the only agency working this case. The thought wasn't a reassuring one, and Grayson wanted to ignore it.

He couldn't. Children's lives were at stake. Families were at stake. Laney's safety was at stake.

He walked back into the kitchen. Laney was still at the table, eyes closed as she said something to Willow. Was she visualizing the perps? Trying to bring their faces into better focus?

Maybe she sensed his gaze. She opened her eyes, glanced his way and offered the kind of smile that seemed to say she was glad he was there.

She was a strong woman, determined, hardworking, energetic and obviously willing to sacrifice her safety for the safety of others.

So why had she retired from search and rescue? His cursory search of national databases hadn't revealed much. She'd retired early from her work, but the article he'd read hadn't said why. He wanted to know. Not because it would help with the case, not because it mattered to the outcome of his investigation, but because he wanted to know more about Laney.

He wasn't sure how he felt about that, but it was a truth he couldn't deny, one that he carried with him as he crossed the kitchen and settled in the chair next to her.

ELEVEN

Laney tried to focus on Willow Scott's work as Grayson took a seat beside her.

It shouldn't have been difficult. Her elegant hands deftly moving across the paper, Willow was bringing Laney's description to life. The work was fascinating, her questions as detailed as her drawing.

Yes. Laney definitely shouldn't have had any trouble keeping her eyes on Willow and her sketch. Unfortunately, Grayson was difficult to ignore. Especially since he'd pulled his chair a little closer, his arm brushing hers as he leaned in to get a closer look at the sketch.

She met his gaze, her heart doing a strange little flip when he smiled.

"So," Willow said, turning the drawing pad toward Laney and forcing her to refocus her attention. "How's this match with what you saw?"

Laney's breath caught in her throat. The charcoal drawing looked like a black-and-white photograph of the gun-wielding kidnapper.

"Wow, that's him." Laney didn't think it could be any more perfect—down to the small scar on his left cheek and the slightly crooked nose. Willow had captured him perfectly.

Grayson leaned over to look at the drawing, his closeness oddly comforting. "I'll run this through my scanner and feed it into the facial recognition system while you work on the sketch of his accomplice."

Carefully tearing the page from her pad, Willow handed it to Grayson. "Let's stretch and grab a drink of water, Laney. Then we'll do the next sketch."

"There's probably some homemade raspberry iced tea in the fridge if you're interested," Laney offered, her focus still on the sketch. The guy looked mean, and she could almost picture him slinking through the kennels, setting fire to her office. Had he been the man on her property? She thought so. And it wasn't a comforting thought.

"That actually sounds good," Willow replied. "I'm a Southern girl at heart, and we do like our iced tea." Willow chatted with Grayson about new updates to the FBI facial recognition system as Laney grabbed the pitcher of tea from the fridge and tried to pour it into a tall glass. Her hands were shaking so hard, the tea sloshed over the sides of the glass, spilling onto the counter.

"Let me help with that," Grayson said, reaching around her, his chest nearly touching her back as he steadied her hand. The tea poured into the glass without a drop spilling, and Laney handed it to Willow, her cheeks warm, her heart racing.

Not because of the sketch. Because of Grayson.

The man was messing with her composure, and she didn't like it.

"Thanks," Willow said, not a trace of Southern accent in her voice. She took gulp of the tea, tilting her head back just enough for Laney to catch a glimpse of a thin scar extending from the bottom of her jaw horizontally across her neck. Even to Laney's untrained eye, it would have been a significant injury. Life-threatening, even. And definitely intentional.

She turned away, not wanting Willow to know she'd been staring.

Whatever had happened, it had been a long time ago. The scar was faded and old.

"Here." Grayson thrust a glass of tea into Laney's hand. "I think you need this. You look a little done-in."

"Gee, thanks," she responded, sipping the tea as she dropped back into her chair.

Willow and Grayson were still on their feet, both of them tall and fit. They looked good together, seemed comfortable with one another. For all Laney knew, they were dating. Good for them. Laney had better things to do with her life than devote it to a man. Her mother had done that. She'd spent her entire adult life trying to please a man who couldn't be pleased. Laney's dad had been a good-looking charmer.

When he wasn't drunk.

Most of the time he was. Behind closed doors, he was a mentally and physically abusive husband and father. Laney had watched her mother lose herself to depression, and she'd vowed never to be in the position where being with someone meant losing herself.

"Okay." Willow's voice jogged Laney out of her thoughts. "I'm ready if you are."

Within an hour, Willow had completed the second sketch. It was eerie how much the charcoal drawing resembled the man. Somehow Willow had even managed to capture his menacing stare.

In the family room, Grayson had set up his portable scanner and laptop.

Jax, Brody and Murphy were lying by the coffee table, watching him work, when Willow and Laney brought him the second sketch.

"This looks great," he said. "I'll get it scanned and entered into the system."

"How long will it take to get the results?" Laney asked.

"That depends. There are thousands of mug shots in the national database. If we don't get a hit there, the system will ping other participating statewide databases according to a query I've set up. This search will run against the California, Boston and Maryland databases first, then hit the rest of the states until all databases are exhausted." He carefully laid the second image down on the scanner. "I'll queue up the next query to run when the first is complete."

The dogs barked, announcing a visitor.

"Place," Laney commanded, going to the door. An overweight, balding man dressed in a blue uniform that read Carlston Construction stood on the threshold. With barely a glance at Laney, he began his practiced spiel. "Good afternoon. I'm here to replace a pane of glass in a window..." he said, flipping through a clipboard of invoices, oblivious to Grayson, who had followed Laney to the door.

"Looks like...back window. Double-paned glass." He looked up, finally seemed to notice Grayson and took a step back. "I do have the right house, don't I?" he asked, looking down at his invoice again.

"We've got a broken window in the back, but I didn't call in an order to have it fixed."

"It was called in by Rose Cantor."

Rose hadn't returned from the kennel. Laney suspected she was camped out in a lawn chair, reading one of her romance novels while Bria tended to the dogs.

A police officer approached the door. "Want me to show him around back, Agent DeMarco?" he asked, and Grayson nodded.

"Yes. Don't let him leave without a guarantee that window will be fixed tonight. It poses a security threat."

"Yes, sir."

The look on the contractor's face had Laney thinking he'd replace the entire window, not just the broken pane of glass, to keep Grayson happy. Of course, she'd be glad to have the window fixed. They'd nailed a sheet of plywood across the window last night, but that brought with it other concerns in case of a fire—a real consideration in light of today's events.

Grayson's laptop dinged twice as they returned to the family room.

Willow looked over at them, a grin spreading across her face. "We have a hit—with a 94 percent accuracy rate, Grayson."

Laney rushed over. Two images—Willow's sketch and a photograph of a convict—were on the screen.

"That's definitely him." She couldn't contain her smile. They had identified one of the kidnappers. That meant they were a step closer to finding the missing children and closing down the child trafficking ring.

"You were the perfect witness, Laney," Grayson said. "I knew you'd be the key to identifying the kidnappers."

"Willow was the key. If she hadn't been able to sketch what I saw—"

"Let's give credit where credit's due," Willow countered. "You managed to really see this guy and commit his face to memory. That's hard to do, even under the best of circumstances. I consider myself fortunate to get a 75 percent likelihood of a match."

"And that's a high average." Grayson added, saving the image to his laptop.

"What do we do now?" Laney asked.

"We put out an APB on David Rallings Jr. Tonight."

The sun was low in the sky, the air crisp. Grayson sat on the porch swing, rocking with one foot. The three dogs had followed him out, and after a brief romp around the yard, they had each found a place on the porch to relax in silence. The windows were open, the aroma of chicken and freshly baked Pillsbury rolls wafting through the screen, mixed with the scent of honeysuckle and pine, nearly masking the now faint smell of smoke. Light chatter and low bouts of laughter came from the kitchen where Laney and Willow were helping Rose prepare dinner.

In any other circumstances, this would have been an idyllic fall afternoon, the evening quiet and relaxing.

He was tense, though, anxious to hear from the local PD. The APB on David Rallings had been issued, and Grayson was hopeful they'd be able to bring the guy in for questioning soon. They had a name, a last known address. And a lengthy criminal record with multiple charges for assault, robbery and domestic violence. He'd served jail time five years ago, but had been clean—or just avoided being caught—ever since. Kent had sent officers to Rallings's house, and they were procuring a search warrant.

Things were coming together.

Unfortunately, there had been no match on the second suspect. They might have an ID soon, though. If Rallings wasn't at his house, if he couldn't be located, both sketches would be released to the media on the ten o'clock news.

The dogs came alert to the sound of tires on gravel, lifting their heads simultaneously, eyes focused on the driveway.

A candy-apple-red 1965 Camaro rounded a curve in the drive.

Arden. Finally.

He loved his sister, but her fear of flying made it difficult for her to move from location to location quickly. But he'd choose her any day over a more accessible computer expert.

She'd driven ten hours, from a contract job in Georgia, to make it to Maryland this morning, heading directly to the precinct to examine their system. He wondered what she'd found, but was certain if something was there, she'd know it. She was a genius, graduating from high school at fourteen and from college with a master's degree by the time she was eighteen. Focused and independent, she marched to her own drum. That was one of his favorite things about her. Unfortunately, along with the genius IQ came some quirks that didn't necessarily endear her to everyone.

She came up the walk, a backpack slung over her shoulder. With her black shoulder-length hair, fair skin and blue eyes, she looked much like their mom.

"Hi, Gray. Mom said to tell you you'll be in hot water if she doesn't hear from you before the week is out." She grinned, stepping into his embrace.

"Is that the way you greet the brother you haven't seen in six months—with threats from Mom?"

"Hey, don't shoot the messenger." She brushed a hand over her hair, sweeping thick, straight bangs from her eyes. It was a new look. One that had probably taken her a year to decide on.

"You look great, kid."

"Flattery won't get you anywhere. You owe me big time, and you know I'm keeping track."

Grayson laughed. "I'm sure you are."

"What's with the dogs?" she asked, bending down to scratch each behind the ears.

"Two of them belong to my witness, Laney. The other is a dog she's training for the MDP."

"Laney, huh? Chief Andrews told me about her this morning. He thinks highly of her."

"I do, too."

"Hmmm…guess I need to meet her, then." With that, she walked into the house without ringing the doorbell or knocking. That was pure Arden. No qualms about walking into other people's space, barely any acknowledgment of the boundaries most people lived inside. It wasn't that she didn't understand the rules. She just tended to ignore them unless it was absolutely necessary to do otherwise.

He followed her into the house and wasn't surprised when she made a beeline for the kitchen. Arden loved cars, computers and food.

Laney and Willow were slathering butter on slices of bread. Rose was tossing a salad. Hopefully she'd had nothing more to do with the cooking. If her burnt cinnamon rolls and mud-like cookies were any indication, the woman should be kept far away from meal preparations.

Inhaling deeply, Arden dropped her backpack on the floor.

"Something smells good. Do you have room for one more?" she asked, taking a seat at the kitchen table before she was invited to do so.

Grayson shook his head.

"Of course there's room," Rose said, setting a plate in front of her. "But get yourself out of that chair and help first. If you want to eat, you've got to work. Get the tea from the fridge and some glasses from the cupboard to the right of the sink."

Laney looked horrified at Rose's barked instructions, and Willow tried hard to squelch her snicker.

Arden laughed outright.

That was another thing Grayson loved about his sister. She knew how to laugh at herself. "Laney. Rose." Grayson gestured toward Arden as she got up to do as she'd been told. "This is my sister, Arden. She's the computer-forensics specialist I told you about."

Laney and Rose smiled in greeting. "Nice to meet you," Laney said. "Make yourself at home here."

"And you remember Willow…" Grayson began.

"Hey, Willow," Arden interrupted. "It's been a while. How's the facial-recognition system working out?"

"Perfectly. Which you know. So stop fishing for compliments," Willow responded with a smile, setting a platter of roasted chicken in the middle of the table.

"Not fishing. Making sure the program I designed works," Arden responded, reaching for a piece of bread and getting her hand slapped away by Rose. "Got paid a lot of money to do it, and I want to be sure the FBI is happy with the return on their investment. I've been toying with some upgrades to speed the processing, mostly by giving it the ability to read multiple file formats without conversion."

"I didn't know upgrades were in the budget." Grayson cut in, trying to steer away from the more technical discussion that was sure to ensue once Arden got on a roll.

"They aren't. I just feel it's not the best product I could have delivered. The first set of upgrades will be on me." Arden tried to snag a cookie from the jar on the counter, and Rose sighed.

"Young lady, we haven't even said our grace yet."

"Oh. Right. Let's do that, then." Arden sat, and everyone else followed suit.

"Grayson," Rose asked as she took a seat opposite him, "would you be willing to do the honors? And if it comes to mind, pray for my niece and her safety. She's too stubborn to listen at times, and we—"

"Rose!" Laney nearly shouted. "Enough!"

"Enough what, dear?" Rose asked with an innocent smile.

"Let's pray," Laney responded, and Grayson was pretty sure she mumbled *before I kill someone* under her breath as everyone bowed their heads.

When he finished praying, he leaned close to her ear and caught a whiff of freshly baked rolls and something flowery and sweet.

"Murder is a capital offense," he whispered, and she choked on her sip of tea.

He patted her back until she stopped coughing and thought about leaving his hand right where it was—resting between her shoulder blades, his fingers just touching the edges of her ponytail.

"So, Laney," Arden said suddenly, her voice a little too loud in the quiet room. "My brother tells me you're a dog trainer."

"That she is," Rose interjected. "Probably the best in the country."

"Let's not exaggerate, Aunt Rose." Laney shook her head.

"No," Arden argued. "Your aunt is right. I thought you might be the Laney Kensington from Colorado, and you are, right?"

"Yes," Laney said, her voice tight, her expression unreadable.

"I've read all about you," Arden said through a mouthful of buttered bread.

"I'm sure there wasn't all that much to read."

"Sure there was. Up until the past couple of years, you were in the news all the time."

Uh-oh. Here she goes, Grayson thought. Arden had a photographic memory…and no filter. "I saw a picture of you, Brody and a family you and your team pulled off the mountain—they ran an article about you being the youngest dog handler on the Colorado Wilderness Search and Rescue Team."

Laney couldn't hide her surprise. "I thought that article only ran locally. Were you a Colorado resident?"

"Oh, no. I liked reading good news stories when I was a kid, so I developed an app that collects and downloads good news from more than three hundred online publications worldwide."

Grayson knew the real reason Arden had developed that application. At thirteen, she'd worried too much about the state of the world—the news stories would keep her up all night. In typical Arden fashion, she'd decided the best way to stop worrying about the bad news was to read only the good. She'd never told anyone but Grayson that, and he'd kept her secret. For her to even admit to the app…she was up to something.

"That must be a lot of reading each day," Willow interjected.

"Surprisingly, no. People would rather read about calamity, so that's what news reporters cover," Arden countered. "Anyway, when I saw that article, I put you and your team into my search engine so I could follow your adventures— they were pretty cool. Volunteers risking their lives to save others. I have tremendous respect for people like you."

"Um, thanks. But I gave that up a couple years ago." Laney's face had gone ashen, but of course Arden wouldn't stop.

"It's a shame. I read that you and Brody had the highest success rate for live finds of any dog-and-handler team in the nation."

"Those stats were probably inflated," Laney responded. "Besides, I retired Brody when he was six—bad hips."

"Do you think he misses the work?" Arden asked.

"At times."

"Do you?"

"No. I lost the passion for it, so it was better I walk away. You have to be on point for wilderness search and rescue. People's lives depend on your ability to stay focused and do your job."

It was a practiced answer, and Grayson wondered what the real reason was.

"What about Jax?" Arden pressed.

"What do you mean?"

"I read he was even better than Brody. Do you think he misses it?"

"Lay off with the twenty questions, Arden. Laney's had a rough couple of days." Grayson figured the direct approach would be the only chance of making his sister realize she was treading on thin ice.

"Sure. No problem." Arden grabbed another piece of bread. "I miss reading those stories, though. They were some of the best. It's a shame that avalanche killed your teammates. Must have been hard on you, huh?"

"I think," Laney said, pushing away from the table, "I'm done." She headed to the foyer.

Grayson got up to follow her.

TWELVE

She needed some air, because she felt like she was suffocating. She unlocked the front door and yanked it open.

"Not the best idea, Laney," Grayson said quietly.

She turned to face him. "I have to check on the dogs."

"You have to stay safe," he responded, opening the coat closet and taking out her jacket. He dropped it over her shoulders, lifting her hair out from under the collar. "So if you need to check on the dogs, I'll go with you."

"You have your sketches and an ID. I'm not necessary to the case any longer, so maybe it's time for me to keep *myself* safe."

"Still grumpy?" he asked.

"No."

"Then I'll just assume my sister's comments upset you."

"They didn't." Not really. It was the memories that upset her. The guilt.

"Arden has no boundaries, but she doesn't mean any harm."

"I know." Laney walked outside.

The sun was just falling below the horizon, golden rays resting on leaves tinged with gold and red. A hint of smoke still hung in the air, mixing with the crisp fresh scent of early fall. That she was there to enjoy the beauty of it was a matter of chance or circumstance. That's what she had always believed, because it had been too hard to believe that the God who had allowed her mother to be beaten and mistreated actually cared about the world or the people He'd created.

Her grandfather had disagreed. Rose disagreed, her years as a missionary in Africa sealing her belief in God's grace and mercy, His direction and guidance.

"You're sad," Grayson said, pressing a hand to her lower back and guiding her down the porch stairs.

"Not really. I just wish…"

"What?"

"That I had the kind of faith you have. The faith Rose has. The kind that says everything is going to be okay. No matter how bad things seem."

"Is that what you think my faith tells me?" he asked, his hand slipping from her back to her waist as they walked side by side. She could almost imagine that they were more than an FBI agent and his only witness. She could almost imagine that he was worth pinning hopes and dreams on, worthy of putting her trust in.

"Isn't it?"

"No." He stopped, urging her around so they were face-to-face. "It doesn't tell me that everything will be okay. It just tells me that no matter what happens, *I'll* be okay. Life is tough, Laney. No matter how strong my faith, no matter how much I believe, that doesn't change the fact that I'm living in a sinful and fallen world. Bad stuff happens." He frowned, touching the very edge of her head wound. "People are hurt. People are kidnapped. People die. I can't stop that from happening, but I can do everything in my power to make sure the people responsible pay for their crimes."

"Your purpose, huh?"

"Exactly." He smiled and started walking toward the kennels again.

* * *

It took two hours to check on the dogs, give them play-time and attention and settle them for the night. It was her normal routine, one she'd carved out of the ashes of her old life. She loved it, but on nights like tonight—with the early fall air touching her cheeks and the crisp hint of winter in the air—she longed to be out on the trail again, working with a team, searching for the missing. Grayson moved beside her as she fed the last dog, locked the last kennel.

"Done?" he asked.

"Yes. It takes a while. I'm sorry if I pulled you from your job."

"Right now, you're my job."

"Your job is to find Olivia and the other children."

"I'm working on that, too."

"Do you think it's really possible they'll be found?"

"I am going to do everything in my power to make it happen."

"If I'd been able to keep them from getting Olivia—"

"Don't," he cut in.

"What?"

"Don't play that 'if only' game with yourself. Regrets don't do anything for anyone. As a matter of fact, they usually just keep us from doing what we could and should and *would* accomplish if we weren't so caught up in the past."

"Did Rose pay you to say that?" she asked, because she'd heard the same thing from her aunt more than once.

"No." He laughed. "Why? Have you heard it one too many times?"

"Maybe."

"Because of what happened with your team?"

She stopped short at his words, her heart slamming so hard against her ribs, she thought it might burst. "That's something I don't talk about."

"Maybe you should," he countered.

"Maybe. But not tonight."

"Okay," he said simply. He didn't say any more. Didn't press her to tell him what had happened. If he asked Arden, he'd get the truth, but Laney doubted he'd ask. She had the feeling that he'd wait until she was ready to tell him.

She liked that about him, the patience, the willingness to allow her to reveal what she wanted when she wanted. She liked *him*.

Moonlight painted the grass gold. Crickets chirped a constant melody. And Laney? She felt oddly at peace. Just for a moment, she allowed herself really to believe that Grayson was right. That everything happened according to God's plan. Her childhood, career choices, and search-and-rescue successes and failures all converging to make her into the person God needed her to be.

And that maybe, just maybe, Olivia was in her path last night for a reason.

And maybe that reason was to bring Olivia and the others home. With hope in her heart, she silently prayed for the strength to see it through.

Laney looked beautiful in the moonlight.

The thought was one that Grayson couldn't allow himself to entertain. Eventually, the kidnapping case would be closed. Laney would no longer be part of his investigation.

And then what?

He knew what he should do. Walk away. Let Laney go her way while he went his.

But there was something about Laney, something that he couldn't ignore. Something he wasn't sure he wanted to ignore.

It had been ten years since Andrea had died. Murdered by a stray bullet that deep down Grayson knew had been meant for him. Her death, a month before their wedding, had been a wake-up call for Grayson. He'd doubted his purpose, second-guessed his career choice. He'd finally come to terms with the reality that his future, his calling, this life he had chosen, did not come without sacrifice. A wife and family of his own were not in his future. He'd been selfish to try to have that with Andrea—a selfishness that had led to her death. He didn't have the time to devote to a family. His job required that he miss birthdays, anniversaries, holidays. That wasn't fair. Not to anyone.

He wouldn't ask another woman to understand the demands of his work, his drive to be successful, not even someone like Laney.

She might understand his single-minded dedication to his work, but she had her own guilt, her own memories, her own reasons for doing the work she did. She didn't need anything else laid on her.

He led her to the sliding glass door, opened it and ushered her inside.

"Gray, is that you?" Arden called from the family room.

"Yes."

"Well, what took so long? I've been done for like... an hour!"

"Have you found anything?" he asked as he and Laney joined her.

Rose was on the recliner, a colorful quilt covering her equally colorful pajamas, nose buried in her devotional. Willow sat on the couch beside Arden, a glazed look on her face. She'd probably spent the past two hours listening to every excruciating detail of Arden's next project.

"Malware," Arden said, her gaze on Gray's laptop. "None of the data you've sent or received via email can be trusted. The malware is very sophisticated."

"Can you disable it?"

"Is there anything I can't do on computers?"

"Way to be vain, sis."

"Vanity is about beauty. I'm confident. But I'll admit,

this is going to take some time. Simply put, someone set up a duplicate email account to intercept all your messages before you received them."

"Can you tell if anything was modified or removed?"

"Unfortunately, no. Because the full files were never saved to your hard drive, not even to your temp files, there is just no way to run a recovery program."

This was bad news. This was Grayson's official FBI email account; he trusted it and the data he received from it.

"Is there any way to tell how long this has been going on?

"I knew you'd ask that." Arden smiled. "It appears the duplicate account was set up about in January."

"So my email has been compromised for nearly a year?" Just about the time he was assigned to the case. Grayson didn't like the coincidence.

"Is there any way to trace who's been accessing the account?" he asked.

"I think so, given time. But until I do, any data you send over this account is in jeopardy. Anything you receive is suspect. You'll have to decide what's more important— to have a secure email account, or to track the hacker on the other end. We can close this account down now, but that means whoever is on the other end will know you're onto him."

"I need to know who's accessing my account." Pacing the length of the family room, Grayson outlined his plan. "I'll call the IT team tomorrow and request a new email account, but will keep this one open. Until I get the new account, I'll do everything the old-fashioned way." He glanced at his watch. "It's too late tonight, but tomorrow I'll call the local PD in California and Boston to request faxes of their case files. I can compare them with versions that were emailed to me."

"You think those files were tampered with?" Willow asked.

"I think there's got to be a reason someone hacked into this account."

He looked up at Laney. "Do you have a fax-machine number I can use, or should I have everything sent to Chief Andrews?

"I have a fax at the reception desk in the kennels. The fire didn't reach there, so it should be fine. Aunt Rose gave you one of my business cards. The number's on it."

"Be careful, Grayson," Arden added. "Make sure you contact someone you trust—otherwise the hard copies may be modified, as well."

"Got it covered."

"There is also the slim possibility that the duplicate account was set up by an FBI system administrator. If that's the case, I won't have much time to complete my forensic investigation—I'd expect him to disable the mirror account, leaving no trace. I'll do what I can tonight, but there is no guarantee I'll be able to track this back."

"Well, Arden," Willow interjected. "it's been great seeing you again, but it sounds like you're planning to work most of the night on this thing and I've got a flight out tomorrow at ten. I think I need to find a hotel room and crash. I caught the redeye last night so I could get here as early as possible, and I'm beat."

Rose looked up from her reading then, glasses perched on her nose, "What's this I hear about hotel rooms when I have a perfectly good cottage just down the drive?"

"I wouldn't want to impose, Rose." Willow said.

"No imposition. I'm staying up here with Laney. My place is a bit smaller, one bedroom. But there's a pullout couch and clean sheets in the linen closet." She stood, folding the quilt neatly over the recliner. "I'll walk you down now. Arden can join you later."

"I'm sure I can find it on my own…"

"I'm sure you can, too," Rose cut her off. "But I need the stretch. I've been cooped up all day and some fresh air will do me good."

Laney frowned. "Aunt Rose, it's too dangerous for you to be walking outside alone right now. Maybe Grayson should—"

Rose sighed. "You young people ought not argue with your elders. Haven't you learned it's futile?"

Arden snickered at Rose's statement.

"Besides, who says I'm gonna be alone?" She started toward the kitchen. "I have two fresh chicken sandwiches and some raspberry tea prepared for the officers out front. I'm sure one of them will escort me down the drive and back in payment for a nice dinner." She emerged from the kitchen, lightweight blue jacket zipped over flowered pajamas, white Keds on her feet and a small picnic basket in her arms. "I threw in some cookies for good measure."

Grayson grimaced. Maybe he should warn the guys before they bit into one of them.

"Of course," Rose continued, "if I had my mace, I wouldn't have to go through the trouble of bribing a police officer with food. Come on, Willow. Let's get out of here."

She was out the door before Willow could make a move to follow.

"Well," Arden said.

"Well, what?" Grayson responded, his gaze on the open front door and on the officers who were being handed chicken sandwiches.

"I like that old lady. She's pretty cool."

"Get back to work, sis." He sighed as Willow walked outside and closed the door.

THIRTEEN

Laney toyed with the idea of sleeping in her very comfortable, yet extremely ugly, fuzzy frog pj's—a Christmas gift from Aunt Rose that, surprisingly, Laney actually used. But she did not want to be seen in public wearing them. Given the last twenty-four hours, she could not even begin to wonder what might interrupt her sleep.

Instead of the fuzzy pj's, she threw on a clean pair of yoga pants and a soft Under Armour T-shirt. Glancing in the mirror, she sighed at her reflection. With her hair pulled back into a loose braid, the staples at her hairline were not quite hidden and still inflamed. Her fair skin, made all the more pale from lack of sleep and worry, only served to accentuate further the unattractive yellowish-green bruise that shadowed her jaw.

It could be worse, she thought wryly, dropping onto the bed. She could be dead.

In the corner of her room, Murphy made himself comfortable between Jax and Brody. No doubt happy that he was not relegated to his usual kennel for the night, the younger dog lay upside down, belly showing, legs in the air, snoring. Head resting on Brody's back and a foot splayed over Jax's, he wiggled in his sleep. Brody let out a huff, but both dogs, friendly to a fault, accepted Murphy— at least for the night.

Good. Laney wanted a peaceful night's sleep. She needed one, because she was starting to think things she shouldn't. Things about Grayson, about her future, about maybe reconnecting with her old purpose, her old mission.

She frowned, touching the old family Bible again.

She wanted what her grandfather and aunt had, what Grayson had.

"Please, just show me what you want me to do," she whispered.

Brody opened one eye, gave a quiet little yip.

She smiled, turning off the light and lying down. She didn't think she'd be able to fall asleep with the events of the past twenty-four hours swirling in her head, but she must have. The next thing she knew, someone was pounding on the door. Loudly.

"Laney? You awake?"

Grayson. She knew the voice, could hear the urgency in it as she tumbled out of bed and across the room, nearly killing herself as she tried to rush to the door. She flung it open. "What's going on? Is it Rose?

"No. Nothing like that."

"Then what?"

"I just got a call from Kent. We finally got the search warrant and entered David Rallings's house."

"Did they find anything?"

"They're still processing the scene, but a car registered to David Rallings Jr. was found on the premises. Inside, the television was blaring, and there was a half-eaten dinner on the table. The front door was open, screen door unlocked. No sign of Rallings or of foul play. Andrews figures that he was tipped off and knew they were coming for him."

"Okay." She wasn't sure why Grayson had thought it necessary to wake her to tell her that.

"There's more, Laney," he said, his expression grim. "Prince George's County Police are reporting a John Doe floating in the Patuxent River. Possible robbery victim. No wallet or ID on him."

Laney knew where this was going, and it wasn't good. "Rallings?"

"He fits the description, but the police haven't been able to find any family to identify him. They'll take prints at the morgue, but it will likely be tomorrow before they can search the databank and get a positive ID. I don't want to wait until tomorrow, Laney. If Rallings is dead, someone is afraid we're getting too close. If that's the case, there's every possibility the kids will be moved sooner rather than later."

"You want me to identify him, don't you?"

"I want you to do what feels comfortable and right. Identifying a body that's been in the water isn't pleasant, and I—"

"I've found drowning victims, Grayson. I've pulled them from rivers and ponds. Older people. Toddlers." They'd been the worst. They were the ones she hadn't been able to forget. "I think I can handle this."

He nodded, glancing at his watch. "I'll meet you in the family room. I need to call Andrews and tell him we'll be at the morgue before midnight."

Laney grabbed her oversize Colorado Search and Rescue sweatshirt from the closet, pulled it over her T-shirt, slipped into her shoes and followed him into the family room. He stood near the window, speaking quietly into his phone.

Arden was still on the couch, Grayson's laptop balanced on her thighs, several devices spread out on the coffee table. She had earbuds in and was bobbing her head to some song only she could hear. She didn't look up as Laney approached.

"Arden?" Laney touched Arden's shoulder, and Arden nearly jumped out of her skin.

"Wow! Man!" She tore the earbud from her left ear. "You scared me."

"Sorry, I just wanted to let you know I'm leaving with Grayson."

"Yeah. He told me," Arden responded, her gaze sliding back to the computer screen.

"I don't want to wake Rose to tell her. If she comes looking for me, can you let her know where I've gone?"

"Sure." Arden replaced the earbud and went back to work.

"Ready?" Grayson asked, shoving his phone into his pocket and taking Laney's elbow. "Andrews said he'll meet us at the morgue in twenty."

"What else did he say?"

"That the security guard who was at the hospital the night of the power outage may have skipped town. His girlfriend called the police to report that he never made it home from work last night. She's suspected him of cheating, so she went straight to the bank to clean their account out. Unfortunately, he'd already been there. Took every bit of the six hundred dollars they had and deposited it into a personal account." He paused as he opened the door and ushered her out onto the porch. "He also transferred ten thousand dollars that she had no idea was there. She was very willing and very able to give us a bank statement. The money was deposited by wire transfer. Half of it twenty minutes before the power outage. The rest after."

"Can Kent trace the transfer?"

"He did. It came from an overseas account. No way to find out who the account holder is. Andrews put out an APB on the security guard. Hopefully we can stop him before he goes too far underground."

"Or before he ends up in the Patuxent?"

"That, too."

The temperature had dropped, and dark rain clouds shadowed the moon. Laney could feel the moisture in the air. There'd be a storm soon. She hoped that wherever

Olivia and the other kids were, they were warm and dry. More than that, she hoped that they'd be home soon. She *prayed* that they would, because she had nothing left but that. No power to change anything, no hope that identifying the body would bring them any closer to stopping the kidnappers. All she had was the feeling that maybe she'd spent her life putting her hope in the wrong things, that maybe she'd spent too much time believing in her own strength and power and not enough time relying on God's.

"Better get in," Grayson said as he opened the passenger door and helped her into his car. "The storm is almost on us."

He closed the door as the first raindrop fell.

The pelting rain made it difficult to drive as fast as Grayson would have liked. Even with the wipers swishing back and forth at full speed, visibility was still impaired. Laney was quiet in the seat next to him, her hands fisted in her lap.

"What are you thinking?" he asked, breaking the silence.

"That Olivia and the other two kids might be out in this mess."

"I doubt the kidnappers would risk the health of their sales product."

"Is that really all those kids are to them?"

"If it weren't, they'd never have taken them in the first place."

"That's sad."

"Lots of things in life are, but there's good stuff too. Like your dogs."

"And your sister."

"And food that Rose doesn't cook," he said, hoping to lighten her mood.

She laughed. "Poor Rose. She has an overinflated opinion of her cooking."

"She's a good lady, though."

"She is. I didn't see much of her while I was growing up. She and her husband were missionaries. She came home on furlough, but it wasn't enough for her to make a difference."

"Make a difference in what?" he asked, turning onto the main highway. They should be only ten minutes from the morgue, but it would take a little longer with the rain. Grayson hoped the medical examiner would stick around.

"My life," Laney said so softly that Grayson almost couldn't hear her. "She's always felt guilty about that. I think it's why she lives in the cottage instead of a retirement home with all her friends. She says she'd be bored there, but I know she'd be happy. Dozens of people around her all the time, plenty of things to do."

"You don't feel guilty about that, too, do you?"

She didn't respond, and he took her silence for assent. "Rose would tell you to get a grip. You know that, right?"

"Rose tells me lots of things. If I listened to all of them, I'd have blond hair and sixteen pairs of bright pink jeggings."

"And twenty of those fuzzy sweaters?"

"Exactly." She shifted in her seat, and he knew she was studying his profile. "Do you think they'll find anything at Rallings's house? Assuming he's dead, there's no hope of questioning him."

"Everyone leaves something behind." How valuable it would be remained to be seen, but Grayson was certain they would find something.

"They killed him because I identified him."

"Guilt again, Laney? Because it's totally misplaced. They killed him because he put their operation at risk."

In the center console, Grayson's phone vibrated, the name Ethan Conrad flashing on the dashboard media system. Grayson accepted the call. "Grayson here."

"Gray, it's Ethan. I got your message but was poring over the files you sent."

"I called to tell you to hold off, Ethan. The integrity of the files has come into question. My system's been hacked."

"Are you sure? Only a skilled hacker could get into the FBI system."

"Arden confirmed it."

"I guess you're sure, then. These guys may be more powerful than either of us imagined."

"I agree."

"It sounds like you're getting close. Be careful." Grayson could hear the concern in Ethan's voice.

"Don't worry, Ethan. I learned from the best. I can take care of myself."

"I know you can, but I think I'll take a trip out that way tomorrow and take a look at the police files on all the cases if you can set it up with the chief. Maybe I could talk to a few people, shake up a few leads."

"I think you'd be wasting your time, Ethan."

"Its possible, but I'd feel better doing something."

"Okay, I'll talk to the chief about it and call you in the morning."

"Sounds good." Ethan paused. "You're like a son to me, and I can't lose another one. Be safe." The connection ended before Grayson could respond.

"He sounds like he cares a lot about you," Laney commented.

"We go way back. He was my best friend's stepfather. Married Rick's mom when Rick was only seven. His own dad walked out on them when Rick was a toddler. Rick idolized Ethan, joined the bureau because of him."

"What happened to Rick?"

"Murdered. It was our first major case. We were both twenty-five. He called me and told me he'd had a breakthrough, but that it wasn't safe to talk over the phone."

Grayson remembered that night like it was yesterday,

the loss of Rick and Andrea on the same day had been a blow he almost hadn't recovered from. He hadn't shared the story with many, but he had the sudden urge to tell Laney. He needed her to know. Understand how dangerous his life really was, not to him, but to those he loved.

"That night I'd picked up my fiancée from the elementary school where she worked. We'd been out for dinner and a movie, celebrating that the wedding planning was done and the date was in less than a month. I was on my way to drop her off at her parents' house when Rick called. He said it was important, sounded frantic. Andrea insisted we go, saying she'd wait in the car and grade some papers while Rick and I talked."

He glanced at Laney. Shadows of rain from the windshield ran over her face, and she looked soft and lovely, but strong in a way Andrea had never been. "When we got there, Rick was nowhere to be seen. I heard the first shot before it hit Andrea. It smashed through the passenger-side window. She fell into my lap, unconscious. Her blood…" He stopped himself. He could still smell the coppery scent of it. "It was an ambush. The second shot broke the windshield, narrowly missing me. The glass shards flew into my face."

"The scar over your eye?" she whispered.

"Yes."

"I drove to the hospital, only two blocks away. Andrea was still breathing, but the damage to her brain was irreversible. Telling her parents was the hardest thing I've ever had to do." They hadn't blamed him. Just cried for their daughter. "Her parents pulled her from life support that evening, after our families had said their goodbyes. She was twenty-three."

Later that night, after she was gone, her father had pulled him aside. *Find who did this to our girl, Gray. Find him and make him pay.*

"I'm so sorry, Grayson."

"I learned later that Rick was dead before we even arrived at the warehouse."

"Did you ever find out who did it?"

"Yes, no thanks to me. I was a basket case, but Ethan stepped in. He examined Rick's case files, traced his cell calls—he solved the case." And he'd made the guilty party pay.

"No wonder this case has him worried," she said.

"It has me worried, too, Laney, but for different reasons."

They fell silent then to the rhythmic cadence of the rain and windshield wipers, each lost in thought.

He glanced in the rearview mirror. In the distance, lights from another vehicle were approaching from behind.

Fast.

Grayson's grip on the steering wheel tightened as he stepped on the accelerator. These weren't ideal conditions for evasive driving, but he'd work with what he had. The old Bowie Race Track was a half mile ahead. Used now as a practice track only, it would be locked up for the night, but he could pull in the drive to let the car pass. If he made it that far.

If not, there was a ditch on one side of the road and the Patuxent River on the other. Neither a good option.

He glanced in his rearview mirror again. The car was approaching at a dangerous speed. They weren't going to make it to the racetrack.

He eased up on the accelerator. One of three things was about to happen. The guy would swerve around them and speed on, he'd slam into the back of the sedan or he'd pull up beside them and fire off some shots.

Better for Grayson to keep his speed down and retain control of the car than for him to try to outrun the vehicle in these conditions.

"Grab my phone, Laney. I want you to call 911."

FOURTEEN

Laney fumbled for Grayson's cell phone, making the call as he navigated the dark, winding road. She glanced out the back window as she spoke to the 911 operator, doing everything she could to keep her voice calm, her thoughts clear.

There was definitely a car behind them. It was definitely gaining fast.

"Don't look back, Laney. Keep your eyes and head forward. Hold on to the armrest."

Controlling her panic, she did what he asked.

"Shouldn't you speed up? He's gaining."

"I will. I'm waiting for the right moment."

Trusting Grayson, she watched the road ahead, the phone falling from her hand as she clutched the armrest and center console.

Grayson's gaze rapidly switched from the road ahead to the rearview mirror and back again. "Here he comes!"

Grayson hit the accelerator and the car lurched forward as the other vehicle slammed into the bumper. The sedan fishtailed, but Grayson maintained control. They were in the center of the two lanes, a curve fast approaching. If another vehicle was coming around the bend, they'd be in serious trouble.

Grayson slowed, getting back in the right lane. "He's coming again."

The impact was stronger this time, the other driver catching on to Grayson's evasive tactics. The sedan accelerated around the corner, Grayson struggling to maintain control. The tires couldn't find traction on the wet pavement. The car spun out, coming to a stop sideways in the middle of the road. The other driver was coming right for them.

Grayson would take the brunt of the impact. "Look out!" Laney screamed.

Grayson stomped on the accelerator, angling the car back into the street and speeding forward just before impact. The other car slammed into the back fender of the much larger sedan.

Pop, pop, pop.

A bullet pierced the rear windshield, exiting through the rear passenger's side window.

Laney heard a fourth gunshot even as Grayson pushed her head to her knees.

"Keep down!" he shouted as he accelerated into the next curve. Two quick shots and the car fishtailed out of control.

"He's taken out the rear tire!"

Laney braced for impact as the sedan careened off the road and into thick foliage.

Grayson struggled to steer the car between two big trees, missing each by mere inches. Laney could only grip the armrest in horror, flinching as branches and leaves smacked the car and windshield. The car jostled down the embankment, sideswiping a large tree and mowing down saplings before skidding sideways, the passenger's side slamming into a fallen tree, air bags exploding.

Grayson looked over his shoulder; Laney followed his stare. The other car's headlights were above them, at the road's edge.

"You have the cell phone?" Grayson asked, his voice calm.

"I dropped it!" She sounded nearly hysterical. She took a deep breath, tried to calm her frantic breathing.

"Check the floor. See if you can find it."

She did what he asked, reaching through pebble-like pieces of broken glass. There! She felt the smooth surface and rectangular shape of the phone.

"Found it!" Laney thrust it into his hands.

As he zipped it into his jacket pocket, Laney shoved at her door with everything she had. "It's wedged against a tree. Does yours open?"

He tried it. "No, it's jammed." He grabbed her hand, squeezed gently. "We'll go out through the window. Hurry."

Cold rain pelted her face and hands as she exited the vehicle and nearly fell headfirst into the roots of the fallen tree. Grayson squeezed out the window after her.

"Where—" she started to ask, but he pressed his fingers over her lips.

"Listen." He breathed the word near her ear, the sound more air than anything.

She froze, tried to hear above the frantic pounding of her heart.

Branches cracked, leaves crackled.

Someone was coming.

Grayson's hand slid from her lips, slipped down her shoulder and her arm until their hands met, their fingers linked. He didn't speak, barely made a sound as he led her quickly away from the car. The pouring rain muffled any noise they made, and she thought that maybe they had a chance of escaping.

There was no light. Nothing to guide their steps. Her eyes tried to adjust to the darkness, but the shadowy trees hid roots and rocks and fallen branches that seemed determined to trip her.

More than once, Laney stumbled over the unforgiving terrain.

They headed downhill, away from their pursuer and

toward the Patuxent River. Rushing water drowned any sound of their pursuer but served to mask Laney and Grayson's progress, as well. Somewhere in the distance, sirens screamed. The police must be on their way.

She wasn't sure they'd arrive in time.

As close as she and Grayson were to civilization, they were cut off from everything.

Grayson pulled out his cell phone, "No signal," he muttered, shoving it back into his pocket. He tugged her close, pressed his lips to her ear, his breath warm against her chilled skin. "When we reach the bend in the river, we'll head up. There's help on the road. I can hear the sirens."

She nodded, clutching his hand as he led her around a curve in the river. From there, they climbed through thick foliage, clutching branches and trees to boost themselves up the steep, rain-soaked ravine.

Leaves had begun to fall for the season, making the ground cover slippery. Laney's feet went out from under her, and Grayson tightened his grip, pulling her back up.

The sound of sirens grew louder, but Laney could barely hear them. She was panting too loudly, her lungs screaming, her head pounding.

She'd thought she'd recovered from her concussion, but her climb up the hill was proving otherwise. What should have been easy was agonizingly difficult, her feet sticking to the ground with every step, her arms shaking as she tried to pull herself up.

Grayson stopped short, Laney bumping into him from behind.

"What—"

"Shh," he cautioned, pulling her around so that they were side by side.

And she saw the problem.

She couldn't miss it.

Eight feet high with six inches of barbed wire across the

top, the chain link fence might as well have been Mount Everest.

"We have to go back," she hissed.

"We have to go over, the race track is on the other side of this fence," he responded, scaling the fence easily and tossing his jacket over the barbed wire. "Come on," he urged, reaching down for her hand.

If he'd been anyone else, she would have said no. If he'd been anyone else, she would have come up with her own plan and trusted it to get her out of the trouble they were in.

But her gut was telling her she could trust Grayson. If there was a way out, he would find it.

She was feeling weak. She wasn't sure she could make it, but she climbed the first few links of the fence and managed to grab his hand.

Behind her, something crashed loudly in the brush.

She panicked, trying to scramble up, her feet slipping from the fence, her body dangling as Grayson clutched her hand and kept her from tumbling down.

"Get your feet back on the fence," he barked, and she somehow managed to do it.

Seconds later, she was beside him, looking straight into his eyes.

"This is the hard part," he murmured, his gaze jumping to some point beyond her shoulder. "I'll go over first, and then I'll help you. If you don't move fast, that barbed wire is going to slice through the jacket and into your skin. Be careful!'

He was over the fence in a heartbeat, and then it was her turn. She grabbed the barbed wire, wincing as it dug into her hands.

"Move fast. The weight of your body is going to sink that barb in deeper if you don't," Grayson encouraged her from the other side of the fence.

She nodded, her brain finally kicking in, all the panic

suddenly gone. She'd done similar acts before, scaling rock walls to find the missing, climbing fences to check ponds and quarries. Only this time, the safety ropes were non-existent, and there was a gun-toting maniac behind her.

The movement in the brush was growing closer, and it was human.

Grayson could hear whoever it was stopping every now and again to listen for signs of its quarry. Laney was scaling the fence more slowly than he would have hoped, but he was mostly relieved she'd made it this far. Her breathing had been labored during their ascent to the fence. It was obvious she was tired. But she never complained. Not one word. She just attempted to stick with him as if her life depended on it.

And it probably did.

Laney precariously straddled the jacket-covered barbed wire.

"Easy…" he cautioned, putting a hand on her arm as she maneuvered her second leg over.

The sound of their pursuer grew louder with every passing moment. He wanted to hurry Laney along, drag her down the fence and onto the solid ground.

If she fell, though, she could break a leg, sprain an ankle, slowing them even further.

She finally got solid footing on the links on the other side of the fence, then reached for the jacket and tugged.

"Just leave it," he hissed. "They're coming!"

"Your phone…" She gave the jacket one more firm tug and it broke free, but the jerking motion sent Laney careening backward.

He grabbed her shoulder, nearly losing his grip on the fence as he caught her.

A branch cracked in the woods on the other side of the fence, and Grayson was sure he saw a sapling sway.

"Let's go!" He scrambled down the fence, then reached for Laney's waist. "I've got you. Drop!"

At once, she released her grasp, falling into his arms, just as a quick pop sent a bullet whizzing by his head.

"Go!" He pulled his own gun, firing off a shot as he shouted for Laney to run. She took off, and he followed, zigzagging through the thick stand of trees that bordered the fence and surrounded the racetrack on all sides. Emerging from the trees, they sprinted across tall grass, coming upon a three-and-a-half-foot wooden railing surrounding the dirt racetrack. Laney was already tumbling over to the other side of it as Grayson reached her.

Across from them, the starting gates and now-rickety spectator stands stood sentry, shadows of a once-popular winter racing venue.

"Hurry. We need to get across the track and find cover. I hope the police heard the gunshots and are heading this way."

They made it to the center of the track, unkempt with overgrown grass and weeds. The footing was uneven in places, holes in the ground threatening to twist an ankle, but they didn't slow their pace until they'd crossed the muddy track again and reached the next wooden rail. By the time their pursuers had cleared the stand of trees, Laney and Grayson were out of range. Grayson could see them racing toward the railing, two dark figures against the gray night.

Ducking behind the empty spectator bleachers, Grayson took stock of the situation. There was really no good place to hide. Every structure surrounding the track allowed entry from too many directions, and with two men after them, that left too many opportunities for ambush.

Beside him, Laney tried to catch her breath.

"Can you make it to the covered horse bridge?" he

asked, pointing to the shadowy structure at the top of the hill, behind the bleachers.

She nodded, pushing a strand of wet hair from her eyes. "I can make it."

"Okay. I'm going to distract them. On my signal, you head for the bridge. Wait for me there. If we can get to the stables on the other side of Race Track Road, we'll have a better shot of getting a jump on them rather than the other way around." Putting on his jacket, Grayson removed his phone. "Take my phone. When you reach the bridge, check for a signal. If you get one, call Andrews and tell him to let the local police know that we're at the racetrack. They're looking for us, but if they don't look in the right place…" He didn't finish. There was no need. Laney knew what was at stake.

The men had already reached the overgrown center of the oval track and were steadily gaining on them.

"Let's give them a reason to proceed with caution," Grayson muttered, taking aim at the lower leg of the closest man. He wanted them alive, because he wanted whatever information he could get from them.

He wanted to live more. He wanted Laney to live.

One shot in the leg, and the guy went down. The other guy dropped too.

"Go!" he commanded Laney, firing a shot at the ground near the second guy's head.

Laney ran, sure that she had a huge glow-in-the-dark target plastered to her back.

At any second she expected to feel a bullet sear through her flesh.

She heard the loud pop of another shot as she reached the wooden bridge. Built nearly thirty years ago, it served as safe passage for Thoroughbred horses and their trainers across busy Race Track Road. The bridge was separated down the middle by a tall fence. Signs marking the exit and entrance gave clear directions to those passing through.

Laney veered to the right, choosing the entrance sign. Since Thoroughbred horses tend to be skittish, there were no windows in the bridge. Completely protected from the elements on all sides with the exception of the entrance and exit, the structure was eerily dark inside. Her footsteps echoed across the dry wood, breaking the silence as she pulled out Grayson's phone, checking for signal. Three bars. Better than none.

Making her way to the other side of the bridge, she dialed Kent's number. A shot rang out, startling her; she could only hope it was Grayson doing the shooting. Heart racing, she peered around the corner of the bridge. Shadows of the now-empty stables loomed directly ahead and to her left, a parking lot to her right. She hit the call button, putting the phone to her ear. It rang once, twice, a third time.

"Please. Please pick up." Laney whispered to the darkness.

"Andrews here."

"Kent, it's Laney."

"Laney, where are you? We expected you twenty minutes ago."

"In the covered bridge on Race Track Road and headed for the stables. We were shot at and our car was driven off the road and into an embankment. We left the car and were followed to the racetrack. We heard sirens close by. I called 911, but I don't think they know exactly where we are."

"Is DeMarco with you?"

"He's trying to keep the gunmen from advancing on us." The words were rushed, frantic-sounding even to her own ears, but she wasn't certain how much time she'd have before she'd need to take off for the stables.

"How many gunmen?"

"Two." Laney lowered her voice. Footsteps pounding on the dirt indicated someone was approaching the bridge. Fast. Was it Grayson or someone else?

"I've got to go. Someone's coming."

She disconnected the call.

Holding her breath and pressing herself into a dark corner of the bridge, she waited, watching the entrance, praying Grayson was the one who'd appear.

Finally, a shadow appeared, tall, broad, moving with a confidence she recognized immediately.

"Thank You, God!" she whispered, rushing to Grayson, throwing herself into his arms.

She wasn't sure who was more surprised. Her or Grayson.

His hands settled on her back, his fingers sliding across her spine.

"You okay?" he asked, his breath ruffling the air near her ear.

"Yes. And I got the call out to Kent."

"Good, but we're not out of danger. One of the guys is wounded, but he and his buddy are still on the move," Grayson whispered, pulling her in the direction of the stables. "If the police know our location, we just have to hold the perps off until help arrives."

Water pooled in small divots and dips in the ground as they left the bridge behind, the saturated ground sucking at Laney's soaked running shoes, leaving an easily traceable impression in the earth.

"We're leaving footprints," she whispered, following Grayson into the first of the two stables in the far corner of the training facility. Smelling of wood and hay, the interior was mostly dry, its windows having been shuttered against the elements.

"I know. I'm hoping they'll follow our tracks into this

stable and waste time searching for us in here—we're
headed out the back and will hide in the next stable over."

Huddling in one corner of the hayloft, arms wrapped
around her legs, knees drawn to her chin, Laney strained
to hear signs of their pursuers. Grayson's jacket, resting
over her shoulders where he left it before taking his place
in a stall below, offered necessary warmth, but she still
shivered slightly with fear. A few minutes ago, the men
had burst into the first stable. She had clearly heard doors
slamming and wood banging, then nothing.

The hayloft, now mostly empty, spanned the middle of
the stable, allowing hay to be thrown down from both sides
into the walkway below. Grayson had placed a loose piece
of plywood in front of her, leaning it against the wall, near
other boards, tools and buckets. From her hiding place,
she was just able to turn her head left and right, having a
clear view of both rear and front of the stable. Below her,
Grayson was hidden in shadows.

The front door creaked open. A man ducked in, pressing himself to the darkened corner of the wall. Remaining
still, Laney controlled her breathing and waited. Grayson
had explained that he wanted to catch one or both men
alive. This was potentially a chance for them to get another lead in the case.

Laney trained her gaze on the man's position. Unmov-
ing, he stood as if waiting. Hair prickled on the back of
Laney's neck, and she turned just in time to see the second
man drop soundlessly through an unshuttered window toward the back of the stable.

An ambush. Did Grayson know?

There was no way to warn him without giving her position away. Laney looked around for something, anything
to arm herself with. Settling on a heavy rubber-ended mallet, she crept from her hiding place to the edge of the loft,

Grayson's jacket sliding soundlessly from her shoulders. Peering down, she kept the second man in sight. A scuffling commotion behind her was met with a gunshot. Then another.

The second man rushed forward, gun drawn. It was probably an eight-foot drop, but Laney didn't hesitate. Pulling herself to a crouching position, hammer in hand, she leapt for him. He caught sight of her at the last minute, trying to duck while pointing his gun at her, but Laney's momentum carried her forward too fast, her knees slamming into his chest. They fell to the ground, his gun clattering against the stable wall, his body cushioning Laney's fall.

She scampered off him, trying to elude him. His calloused hand grasped her wrist, pulling her back toward him. Hammer in hand, she turned, intending to bring it down on his head. Raising his forearm, he blocked the blow, yelling in pain as the hammer smashed against bone.

Behind her, a gun exploded, its echo merging with the sound of screaming sirens. Outside the stable, car doors slammed and a dog barked.

Help had finally arrived.

Grayson rushed forward, yanked Laney back, and pointed his firearm at the attacker. "Don't move!"

In that moment, both the front and back doors of the stable burst open.

"Police. Drop your weapons!"

Laney froze, dropping her mallet.

"FBI!" Grayson shouted, throwing one hand in the air and slowly placing his gun on the ground. "Don't shoot!"

Kent Andrews and five officers converged on the scene, guns drawn.

"You two okay?" Kent asked, his gun trained on the man who lay on the floor.

"Barely," Grayson muttered, lifting his gun from the ground.

That's when the gunman moved, his hand snaking out as he reached for his weapon.

"He's going for his gun!" Laney cried.

The guy rolled to his side, the gun clutched tightly in his hand, his eyes gleaming.

Grayson shouted Laney's name, tackling her to the ground as the first bullet flew.

A quick succession of returned fire from the officers ended before Laney and Grayson had even hit the ground.

FIFTEEN

The rain had subsided, leaving in its place a cold chill that permeated the thick evening air. Grayson felt it to his bones as he led Laney out of the Prince George's County Morgue.

Despite the jacket he'd thrown over her shoulders, she was shivering violently, her teeth chattering as they walked into the parking lot.

He'd managed to keep her from being shot. Barely.

Grayson was worried. With three dead suspects, a probable arsonist on the run, a stolen car and one jailbird refusing to sing, Grayson was pinning his hopes on the idea that the search of David Rallings Jr.'s residence would yield some new clue. "You doing okay?" he asked, and Laney nodded.

"Aside from being half frozen to death, I'm fine."

"I may be able to help you with that," he responded, and she eyed him dubiously.

"If you're talking about a repeat of that hug—"

Her comment was so surprising, he laughed. "I wasn't, but now that you mentioned it, I don't think I'd mind a repeat performance."

"Grayson—"

"Tell you what," he said, reaching Andrews's police cruiser and popping the trunk. "How about we just worry about getting you warm?" The chief had given him the keys and told him that he and Laney could wait in the car.

It had been as obvious to him as it had been to Grayson that Laney was at the end of what she could handle. She'd identified the deceased, answered a couple of dozen questions. Now she needed to be bundled up in a blanket and left alone.

Grayson grabbed a blanket from the emergency kit in the back of Andrews's car and wrapped it around her shoulders.

She didn't speak as he opened the passenger door and eased her into the front seat.

"Laney?" He touched her hand. It was ice-cold, her complexion so pallid he was surprised she was still conscious.

"I told you, I'm fine." But her voice broke, and she turned away, a single tear sliding down her cheek.

He closed the door, then walked around the car, slipping into the driver's seat.

Grayson started the car and got the heat going, then turned toward Laney.

"It's okay to cry after you see something like that."

"I'm not crying." She swiped another tear from her cheek.

"Your eyes are just leaking all over your face?"

"Something like that," she responded with a trembling smile.

"Do you want to tell me why?" he asked.

"I like you, Grayson. You know that?"

"You sound surprised."

"Maybe I am. I guess I didn't expect to…" She shrugged.

"What?"

"Ever meet someone who was as passionate about what he does as I am about what I do. You were great tonight. Calm and smart."

"Not smart enough. Both our perps are dead. I wanted to bring them in alive."

"I'd rather have you alive. And me." She shivered and tugged the blanket closer around her shoulders.

"You didn't answer my question," he prodded.

"About why I'm crying? I guess it's because three men are dead. They weren't good men, but they were human beings. And I guess it's also because I'm worried that their deaths mean we'll never find Olivia and the other children."

"It's not your job to find them," he reminded her gently, taking her hands, holding them between both of his, trying to warm them.

"Maybe it is, Grayson. If I had a location, I could take Jax and we could—"

"Laney, you don't have to be the responsible one all the time."

"I don't know how to be any other way," she replied softly.

"How about, just for now, you close your eyes and trust me to take care of the situation? I won't let you down." Even as the words rolled off his tongue, he knew he shouldn't have said them. He couldn't make any promises or guarantees. Not even for a night.

But deep down, he felt the need to say them. He wanted her to feel safe. More than that, he wanted to protect her. The alternative was unthinkable.

Chief Andrews rapped on the glass near Grayson's head, and he opened the door and got out. "Everything taken care of?"

"The medical examiner is getting prints from the deceased. Neither was carrying identification." Andrews looked tired, his eyes deeply shadowed. "I'll get you two back to Laney's place. She needs her rest. I'm afraid you'll have to ride in the back."

"No problem." Grayson slid into the back of the cruiser.

"You have any idea who knew you were coming out

here tonight?" Andrews asked as he pulled out of the parking lot.

"Could have been someone at your office. Could have been someone with the FBI. Which means we're right back where we started."

"I just don't get it. The shooter is dead. The accomplice can't be identified through the facial recognition system. And even if we find a match later, the damage is done. Laney's already given us all the information she knows. Why continue to try to harm her?"

"I don't think it's just about Laney anymore. I believe we're getting close to the guy who's calling the shots. He's trying to buy time whatever way possible."

"You could be right," Andrews agreed. "If they can take out the lead investigator and the only material witness to the crime at the same time, the investigation could be set back a day or two."

"Just enough time to get the required number of children needed for the next delivery and stick with the pre-arranged shipping plans," Grayson said.

"It's also possible there's something significant in Rallings's place. We've got someone looking through his computer files now."

"I'm really hoping you're right, Andrews. But either way, I have a feeling we're on the verge of breaking this case wide open."

The ride home was short and, thankfully, uneventful. The house was dark as they pulled up to it. A patrol car guarded in the driveway. A black sedan was also in the driveway, its occupants concealed behind tinted windows. The FBI protection detail had arrived.

Laney didn't wait until Grayson and Kent got out of the car. She opened her door and hurried up the front steps.

The door opened before she reached it. Arden stood silhouetted in the opening.

"Looks like you lived," she said without preamble.

"Yes. I guess we did." Laney sidled past her, the dogs wagging their tails happily as she entered the house.

"I heard all about it on the news. Crazy stuff. Bullets flying and two people dead. Called the chief to see if you and Grayson were involved. Glad it wasn't you or my brother in those body bags." She retreated to the couch and the laptop, shoving earbuds back in her ears.

Laney left her there. She wasn't in the mood for conversation. She was tired and cold. Thankfully, Rose was in bed, her door closed. Laney crept past the guest room and walked into her own.

Jax followed her, dropping down on the floor near the foot of her bed. She knelt down, putting her arms around his furry neck. He whined softly, and she knew he sensed her mood, felt the same need for action that she did.

"For someone who's nearly frozen, you move fast," Grayson said from the doorway.

"The car ride warmed me up."

"And what didn't get warm from the ride, Jax is taking care of?" He sat down next to her on the floor, his body close enough that she could share his warmth too. "He's a good-looking dog."

"I think so. The pick of the litter, and a gift from a team member." Remembering eight-week-old Jax brought a smile to her face. "Jeremy's mom bred Aussies. Jax's play drive was so good, even at eight weeks old, that Jeremy convinced his mom to let me have him."

"That was a generous thing to do."

"Yes. It was. She still sends me Christmas cards every year, and I send her pictures of Jax on his birthday."

"No pictures for Jeremy?"

"Jeremy died two years ago." She was quiet for a minute after that, thankful that Grayson didn't interrupt the silence, that he let her have the time to pull her thoughts together. It gave her the strength to continue. "We were best friends all through college, and he joined me in search-and-rescue training because he was jealous of the time I spent there. He was the flanker on my team. One of the best I ever had. Later he qualified with his own dog."

"Sounds like a good guy."

"He was."

"And after he died, you didn't want to work search and rescue anymore."

"I didn't, but not just because of him." She hesitated. This wasn't something she spoke about. Ever. But Jax's warm weight rested against her left side and Grayson's warm presence was to her right, and the words just spilled out. "I lost two other team members that day. It shouldn't have happened. We were on a routine search—three hikers had been reported lost on the peak. The conditions were good for a find that day. The temperatures were relatively mild."

It had started like any other search. Working with local law enforcement, she'd mapped the search sectors based on the victims' supposed area of travel. "Tanya and Lee were Jeremy's flankers that day. Ironically, when I mapped the sectors, I took the steeper, more treacherous sector because Tanya was three months pregnant and tired a little more easily. I was working the east perimeter of my sector, which bordered Jeremy's sector, when I heard the first rumbling echoes of the avalanche. I called a warning to the team and base," Laney's voice broke. "But it happened so fast, not everyone was able to clear the area."

His arm slid around her shoulders, and he pulled her closer to his side. "You can't blame yourself for that."

"I try not to, but there's no one else to blame," she responded, her hand lying on Jax's soft head, her head resting against Grayson's shoulder.

"There is no one to blame. Nature is a hard taskmaster. There isn't a search-and-rescue professional alive who doesn't know it."

He was right. Her head knew it, but her heart was a different story.

Taking a breath, she fought to control her emotions, still raw after all this time. "It's easy to say when it isn't your team. I've heard it from everyone, and I still can't forget that I was the one who put them in that position and that I lived while they died."

"I don't think they would want things to be different," Grayson said, smoothing hair from her cheek, his fingers warm against her skin. "As a matter of fact, if they were standing in your shoes, if they were the ones who'd lived and you'd died, they'd be mourning your loss, wishing they could have taken your place."

"But they aren't here, Grayson," she said, and the tears she'd been holding back spilled out. "I am, and I can still remember every minute of the search, every second that ticked by in my head. I can remember digging them out and trying so desperately to breathe life back into them." Laney wiped the tears from her eyes, but the vivid memory of that day stayed with her, a picture in her mind, unblurred by her tears and not lessened by time.

Grabbing Laney's shoulders, Grayson turned her to face him, pulling her into a silent embrace. The soft scent of rain and pine trees mingled with a hint of aftershave. Relaxing into him, her tears fell freely. Tears for Jeremy, Tanya and Lee. Tears for herself. For the first time, she let someone else share the enormous weight of their deaths. Not just anyone, but Grayson. A stranger to her a mere day ago, yet her life was now inexplicably tied to his.

"Do you think I don't understand?" he asked gently.

"After Andrea died, everyone told me it wasn't my fault. That everything would be okay. But the truth is, I knew it wasn't my fault. And yet I couldn't help feeling her safety and well-being were my responsibility. I had promised her forever when I gave her that ring, and we never got a chance to start our lives together—to raise the children she always wanted. It wasn't okay. Her death will never be okay. There will always be a place in my heart for her, and I'll always carry regrets. But I've learned to give them to God. Not to dwell on them. Not to lie in bed at night, reliving that day, playing the 'what if?' game. I've grown stronger through her life and death—Andrea wouldn't have wanted it any other way."

He pulled back and looked into her eyes, gently brushing tears from her cheeks.

"You honor your friends every day by your strength, your kindness and your life. Let God bear the burden of their deaths while you rejoice in what you shared together. The good times. Not the bad ones."

Looking into his ocean-blue eyes, Laney could almost believe that was possible.

SIXTEEN

Morning came quickly. The antique grandfather clock in the corner chimed 6:00 a.m., but a soft clatter from the kitchen and the scent of coffee brewing told Grayson he wasn't the first to wake. Yawning, he rose from the couch and stretched. Some coffee would do him good. He'd had a restless sleep, haunted by nightmares and memories, and by the nagging feeling that he was missing something.

He'd spent a couple of hours looking through his files again, familiarizing himself with every word, making a list of every cataloged clue, every person who'd worked on each case, every interview, hoping that when the originals were faxed to him, it would be easier to pick out deleted information. He'd start making phone calls to Boston and California this morning, both local PD and the original FBI case agents. Hopefully he'd have the files in his hands this afternoon.

In the kitchen, Rose looked up from her task of pouring herself a cup of coffee.

"Here." She held the cup out. "It looks like you need this worse than I do. I'll pour myself another."

"Do I look that rough?"

She laughed, green eyes twinkling. "Well, let's just say you look as if a good, strong cup of coffee and a shower wouldn't hurt."

"Well, what a coincidence, because I was just thinking about both."

"Were you thinking about a slice of coffee cake? I've got some right here."

He hesitated, and she laughed again. "No worries, Gray. It's not homemade."

"I wasn't—"

"Of course you were." She cut a slice of coffee cake and put it on a plate. "Everyone who knows me knows I can't cook. I'm not one to give up, so I keep trying. Plus—" she looked around and lowered her voice "—I love to see the expressions on people's faces when they bite into something I bake. And watching them try to dispose of the food while I'm not looking? Priceless!"

"You're incorrigible, Rose," he said, sipping the coffee and letting the hot, bitter brew wipe away some of his fatigue.

"I am," she responded. "But I like you. So I won't make you eat any more of my homemade treats."

"Do I smell coffee?" Laney came around the corner into the kitchen, dressed in her work gear, hair pulled back in a high ponytail. Jax, Brody and Murphy were at her heels.

"Good morning, love," Rose said cheerfully. "I just made a pot, and I've got coffee cake to go with it. Fresh from Safeway. That sweet little Willow took my car and bought some groceries last night. There are a lot of mouths to feed in this house."

"You're up early, considering you didn't get to bed until after one this morning," Grayson commented as Laney sat at the table.

"You're one to talk," she countered. "You were still clicking away on your computer when I finally dozed off."

He nodded to concede the point. "What are your plans for today?"

"Bria is coming by this morning to help with the dogs. I

need to run the board-and-trains through their paces today. I really don't like skipping a training day. I told Riley to take a few days off." Adding a generous portion of cream and sugar to her coffee, she took a sip. "You?"

"Well, after last night's incident, I don't have a car. The FBI is supposed to send me another one when the protection detail shift change occurs. But you're stuck with me until then."

The back door slid open and Arden entered, carting a backpack full of equipment and her laptop. Dropping her bags on the ground by the table, she barely remembered to say hello before starting in. "Is there any coffee cake left, Rose? I tried a piece last night, and it was delicious. Since my brother is a pig when it comes to things like cake, I thought I'd better hurry over before he finished it."

"I'm surprised *you* didn't finish it off last night, Arden," Grayson said as Rose placed a piece of coffee cake on a plate in front of her.

"I would have," Arden said, "but Willow told me she'd cut off both my hands if I touched it again before morning."

"You left for Rose's cottage before Laney and I were done talking, so I didn't get a chance to ask you what you found."

"Well, I haven't identified the hacker yet, but I'm pretty sure he's a hacker for hire."

"How do you know?" Grayson was almost afraid to ask since it was early, and Arden's technical speak could be quite off-putting at times.

"Well, he used some very sophisticated binary obfuscation techniques to prohibit reverse engineering that could identify the original malware commands and potentially lead to his identity. Fortunately for you, I'm familiar with all of the techniques used. Even more fortunately for you, one of the techniques can be traced to only four people in the world."

"How could you possibly know that?"

"Because I created it, and I limited distribution with a signed nondisclosure agreement."

Grayson was starting to get excited—he didn't know much about binary obfuscation or reverse engineering techniques, but he understood that the pool of potential hackers just got a whole lot smaller. "So, are you telling me that we can narrow the hacker down to three people?"

"I'm telling you we can narrow the release of the technique to three people. One could be the hacker, but it is just as feasible that one of them could have sold the technique illegally, in violation of the ten-year nondisclosure agreement."

"Well, that still seems promising."

"It is. I need to analyze my findings this morning, and I should have a name for you early this afternoon."

Getting up from his chair, he hugged Arden, then kissed her on the cheek. "Way to go, kid. I knew you would come through for me." His sister blushed under his public display of affection.

"Don't blow it out of proportion, Gray. You know Mom would kill me if I left you hanging—and Dad might help."

"I love you, too, sis." he countered, winking.

Winking back, she polished off the last bit of her slice of coffee cake. "All that late-night work sure did build up my appetite, Rose. I don't suppose you'd mind giving me another piece of that cake?"

Rose snorted, cutting another slice and placing it on Arden's plate. "Are you ever not hungry, child?"

"No. I don't think so."

Grayson laughed, stretching. "The apple definitely didn't fall far from the tree. Everyone in our family likes to eat. I'm going to hit the shower."

He turned to Laney, leaning down so that he could speak close to her ear. "Wait for me before you head to the kennels. I'll only be a minute."

* * *

Grayson's "minute" turned into thirty. Good thing Bria wasn't scheduled to arrive until seven.

Laney sipped her second cup of coffee, picking at the coffee cake that Rose had set in front of her. She wasn't hungry, but she knew she needed to eat. She had a lot to do, and doing it without nourishment would be foolish.

"My brother thinks highly of you," Arden said through a mouthful of toast. "What do you think of him?"

"Not very tactful, are you?" Smiling, Rose sipped her coffee. Then she turned to Laney. "But, since I'm curious, too, I won't chastise you for it."

A blush crept into Laney's cheeks. The answer should be simple, really. She hardly knew Grayson. He was obviously a good agent. A man of strong faith. A solid, dependable person willing to put his life on the line for her. She should feel respect for him—and nothing more.

"Umm…I think he's great?" It came out as a question. Stuffing her mouth with a bite of the coffee cake, Laney hoped to avoid another uncomfortable question.

"Good." Arden smiled with a conspiring glance at Rose.

Laney didn't like the direction she thought this conversation was about to take. It was hard enough to get the upper hand with Aunt Rose, but Laney suspected Arden would give her aunt a run for her money. She was thankful when a knock at the door set the dogs off. She excused herself to answer it.

"Good morning, Laney. Is Grayson up?" Kent asked, stepping into the house.

"He's in the shower."

"Not anymore." Grayson rounded the corner of the hallway, towel-drying his hair and carrying his dirty clothes. "What's up, Andrews?"

"There's been a development. I'm on my way to the scene of a possible kidnapping. The MO is different, but

I'm not taking any chances. Deputy Wallace is en route, and I've got units dispatched. We've called in the Greater Maryland Region Search and Rescue Team. Since you're not due to get your replacement vehicle until later this morning, I thought I'd check to see if you want to ride along."

"I'm not sure I'm comfortable leaving Laney here."

"You need to go," Laney cut in. There was no way she wanted him babysitting her when he should be out in the field rescuing an abducted child. "I'll be fine. There are two FBI agents and two officers outside."

Grayson hesitated, then nodded. "Okay. Tell me what the situation is, Andrews."

"A group of fifth graders was on an overnight field trip at Arlington Echo last night. Four kids woke up before their chaperone and snuck out to find some poison ivy to shove in another kid's shoe."

"Nice," Laney said.

"Yeah. Not. One of the kids, ten-year-old Carson Proctor, got separated from his buddies. They were calling to him, trying to help him find the way back, when he started yelling for help. The other kids saw him being carted off into the woods."

"Arlington Echo is more than two hundred acres of forest," Laney said. "The kidnapper was on foot. He could still be out there with the boy. How many resources is the search and rescue team bringing?"

"Unfortunately, they have only two deployable dogs in the state right now. Seems the rest of the team is in New Jersey at the National Search and Rescue Conference. My guys are going to act as flankers since there's no telling if the guy is armed," Kent responded.

"Two dogs are not enough dogs to cover all that ground."

"We're calling other teams in the area, Laney. It's just going to take time to get them here."

"We don't have time," she responded, her heart thudding painfully.

Laney knew what she had to do, but she was almost too scared to say it.

She took a deep breath, thinking about what Grayson had told her. She couldn't keep mourning her team members' deaths. She had to start celebrating their lives. The best way to do it was to carry on with the work they'd been doing when they'd died. "I'm bringing Jax out of retirement."

"Since when?" Grayson asked, his gaze sharp.

"Since right this minute." She opened the hall closet, pulling out an orange Coaxsher search and rescue pack. "I've got my ready pack here. I just need to fill the water bladder and I'll be set to go." She did it quickly, ignoring her aunt's questioning look and Arden's incessant chatter. Ignoring Grayson's worried look and Kent's excited one.

"Tell Bria I was called away, Aunt Rose. Tell her to feed the dogs. I'll be back when I can."

Laney grabbed a red lead off a hook in the closet.

The situation was critical. They needed to find the child, and the kidnapper, and they needed to do it quickly. Laney was pretty sure that if they missed this opportunity, it might be too late for Olivia and the rest of the children as well.

But she was scared out of her mind, terrified that she'd make a wrong decision, cause someone to be injured or killed.

She had to trust herself.

No. She had to trust God. He'd see her through this.

She wanted to believe that.

She would believe it.

"Jax, come."

Jax darted to her and sat at her feet, immediately giving her all his attention. Fastening the lead on his collar, she looked at Murphy and Brody.

"Sorry, boys, not today." Then she followed Grayson and Kent out to the patrol car.

The patrol-car sirens and lights were blasting as the cruiser sped down Route 2 toward Arlington Echo. The FBI detail was ill-equipped for a search, so they stayed behind to watch for signs of trouble at the house. Laney was quietly looking out the window as the scenery whizzed by. Jax, his head resting on her lap, was sprawled across the backseat. Laney absently petted his silky ears.

Grayson wondered what Laney must be feeling, headed to a search for the first time since the avalanche. From the tension in her face, he guessed whatever she felt, it wasn't good.

They reached Arlington Echo in under ten minutes and pulled into the lot where a table had been set up as a base. To Grayson, the scene looked a little disorganized, perhaps even chaotic. There were children, camp counselors and adult chaperones standing around the perimeter of the woods behind a line of bright orange flagging tape. Men and women in uniform stood near the table and milled around the parking lot.

They were waiting for direction, and apparently Laney planned to be the one to give it.

She jumped out of the car and hurried to the table. She had a compass hanging from her belt, along with a map pouch and a bottle of what looked like baby powder.

It took her about ten seconds to get people organized.

Two other dog handlers were suddenly at the table, photocopied pictures of the missing boy in their hands, listening as Laney explained how they'd sector off the area.

Grayson watched with interest as the dog handlers studied their maps, jotting notes on pads small enough to stuff in the pockets of tactical pants.

Andrews approached the group, giving clear-cut rules for engagement. They weren't just dealing with a missing child. They were dealing with a kidnapper.

The chief gave out the assignments. "Sector one is for team one, composed of Kensington, DeMarco and Reese. Sector two is team two with Collins, Gentry and Pinkerton. And sector three is team three with Henderson, Graft, Wilfred and Davis. Any questions?"

"Which comms channel will you broadcast from?" The question was asked by a member of the volunteer search and rescue team.

"Set your radios to channel two. Maintain radio silence as much as possible. The suspect doesn't want to be found. If he hears you, he will go into hiding—or worse, he'll go for an attack. You need to be clue-aware, look for fresh tracks, articles of clothing, anything that could belong to our suspect or victim. Okay, unless there are any questions, I need you to get started," Andrews said, dismissing the group.

Grayson made his way over to Laney. She'd spread out her map on the car hood and was marking a point on it. Glancing over her shoulder, he could see she had drawn a circle for base. "Looks like I'm with you," he said.

"Can you find our other team member? I think his name is Reese. I want to go over our search strategy and get started quickly."

"I'm right here." An armed parks and recreation officer approached, a small pack on his back. He introduced himself, "I'm David Reese.

Laney stepped forward, extending her hand. "Pleased to meet you. I'm Laney Kensington. This is Grayson DeMarco. Have you had any prior search experience with dog handlers?'

"No, ma'am, but I've been on wilderness searches before without dogs."

"Good. There are three things to remember. First, don't pet or feed the dog when he's got his vest on. Second, keep up. And third, never get between the dog and the handler. Understand?"

Grayson and Reese nodded.

"Cool." She smiled, and Grayson could see that she was in her element, completely comfortable with what she was doing. "Take a look at this map. This is our sector. We'll check the wind when we get closer, but at first glance I'm inclined to follow this stream, because the terrain is relatively flat compared with the surrounding areas. With a seventy-pound kid in tow, the kidnapper will likely be looking for the path of least resistance." Laney folded the map and put it in her plastic map case, then used her compass to orient her map. "There's bottled water at the base. Both of you grab some. We'll be traveling fast, and you'll become dehydrated quickly. I'll vest up Jax, and we'll get moving."

SEVENTEEN

It felt like coming home.

Every detail of the preparation, every whiff of pine needles and outdoors, every sound of dogs barking and people calling to one another felt as comfortable as a well-worn cardigan.

Laney led the way through a small clearing, moving into the tree line and the edge of their sector. She knew where they were heading, but she paused there to orient her map once more.

Beside her, Jax was visibly excited. He knew this wasn't just training. He always knew. She'd never been sure if it was because he was so in touch with her moods, but Jax's entire demeanor was different on a real search than during a training exercise.

She bent over, scratching him between the ears. "We're about to start, buddy. Just need to do one thing first."

Shrugging the pack from her back, she dug into the front pocket, pulling out a Leatherman.

"What are you doing?" Grayson asked, leaning over her as she opened the knife.

"I need to cut the bells off Jax's vest. They'll give him away if the kidnapper is in our sector. Jax works fast and he ranges, so he'll be out of our sight sometimes. I use the bells to help me keep track of the direction he's traveling and the area he's covered. This time, we'll work without them." She sliced off the bells and stuffed them deep into her pack. Finally they were ready.

Her pulse raced, her heart tripping all over itself.

This might be like coming home, but that didn't mean she wasn't nervous about it. She took a deep breath, removed Jax's lead and placed that in her pack as well.

"Are you ready, Jax?"

He snuffed his agreement, tail wagging his excitement. "Go find!"

At the search command, Jax was off, into the woods and out of sight.

Laney took off after him, Grayson and Reese two steps behind.

The trees offered plenty of shade from the early October sun, but the Maryland humidity was heavy, and it was tough navigating through the dense, thorny underbrush. They'd walked less than three minutes before coming upon the stream that served as a natural border for their sector. Jax was relentless in his work, making large circles around handler and flankers, nose to the air as they moved quickly forward, Laney leading them on with quiet confidence. Grayson was amazed at the speed at which they were covering ground.

But he was still worried that they weren't moving fast enough.

The kidnapper was on the run. It had been nearly forty minutes; if he was not already out of the woods, he was nearing the road, slowed only by what must feel like the growing weight of a child. After all, seventy pounds of dead weight would be challenging for anyone to cart through brush and over uneven ground as the heat and humidity of the day settled in the woods. Surely he would have to stop and rest.

Of course, if he had a weapon, he'd likely be forcing the child to walk through the woods himself, but then they'd have to go at the pace of a frightened ten-year-old.

Laney put her hand up. "Wait."

Grayson and Reese stopped dead in their tracks.

Laney's complete focus was on Jax.

"What is it?" Grayson asked

"He's caught scent. It's faint—I can tell he can't pinpoint the origin." Laney pulled her GPS from the large pocket of her cargo pants, "I'm marking the spot where Jax first showed interest." She released white powder from her puff bottle into the air. "The wind is pushing the scent across the creek. It's hitting the side of this hill and circling up. Scent forms a cone of sorts, stronger near the person and weakening as it gets further away, but sometimes the air movement can push it into a barrier where it gets trapped, leaving a heavy scent pool with no subject. This is when the handler has to read the dog and use whatever scent theory they know, and try to work out where the subject might actually be."

"What are you thinking?" Grayson asked. Could the kidnapper be somewhere close by, hiding until they passed?

"I think he's either picked up the kidnapper and victim, or he's picked up the scent of another dog team working the other side of the stream." Reaching for her radio, she called base.

"Go ahead, team one."

"Permission to go direct with team two."

"Team one, you have the frequency."

"Team two from team one."

"Go ahead, team one."

"Jax is picking up scent on the border of my sector. It's faint. Judging by the air current, my best guess is it's coming from across the stream in your sector. Are you working in the vicinity?"

"Negative, team one. We're at the west end of our sector, near the lake."

"Copy. To be sure he's not picking up our victim or the perp, I'm going to cross the stream to see if the scent pool is stronger. I'll probably go about fifty meters in. If he picks up scent, I'll follow. If not, I'll return to my sector. I'll let you know when I've left the area."

"Copy, team one."

Holstering her radio, she backtracked about fifteen paces, checking the wind, then headed to the stream.

"Jax, this way." Looking over her shoulder, she gestured to Grayson and Reese. "Guys, stay close. Keep your eyes and ears open. My gut is telling me someone is across the stream, just upwind of us. Could be a random hiker, but one thing is certain. It's not a member of the search team."

Grayson and Reese followed single file behind Laney and Jax as they crossed the ankle-deep stream. The water, somewhat cloudy after the rain, moved swiftly over slippery rocks and a muddy stream bed.

Jax paused, lapping up some of the cool water. Bending down, Laney splashed the water under his belly. "Okay, this way Jax, go find!"

Jax paused, his head popped up in interest, nose to the wind, and he was off. Laney went after him, keeping up a fast jog over uneven ground, dodging tree branches and ripping away from thorny brush that reached out to grab her as she passed. Unencumbered by a pack, Grayson stayed on her heels. Reese fell back slightly, Laney's pace combined with the weight of his pack proving too much for him.

For a moment they lost sight of Jax. Laney stopped abruptly, motioning for them to do the same. The distant sound of the dog jumping quickly through the brush was met with another sound.

Something large was moving in the same general direction.

All at once, the second movement stopped, and the distinct sound of the dog running toward them grew closer.

Standing stock-still, Laney waited. Seconds later, Jax bounded into view, tongue lolling, ears back, at a full sprint. Launching himself in the air, straight at Laney, his front paws hit her in the torso before he landed in front of her, tail wagging.

"Show me!" Laney commanded, and Jax quickly started off again.

All three raced after Jax, crashing through the vegetation, jumping over downed branches. But there was no way they could keep up with the agile little Australian shepherd. It seemed to Grayson that Jax was well aware of this. He constantly circled back, ensuring Laney was right behind him.

Bursting through thick underbrush into a clearing, Jax stopped, then began circling the area—nose to the wind, taking in short quick snuffs of air.

"Grayson." Laney's voice was hushed. "The subject was here, but has moved. He's likely hiding. Jax is trained for this scenario—we sometimes see it with lost children and Alzheimer's patients. They are found by the dog and then move before we can get to them."

Fascinated, Grayson watched Jax work. The dog sniffed the ground, the trees, the air, looking for the scent. Even untrained, Grayson could tell when he found it. His head popped up again and his tail fanned out. In a flash, he was off. They followed him through a particularly thick stand of trees and brush and watched as he approached a large downed tree, its exposed roots jutting out, nearly four feet high in places.

A perfect hiding place.

Scampering up the downed trees limbs, Jax was quickly up and over the obstacle. Laney seemed poised to follow, but Grayson grabbed her arm, jerking her back toward him. He was about to have her call Jax back when a shot rang out.

Was Jax shot? Was he hurt, confused? Looking for her?

She had to get to him. Laney tried to shrug free of Grayson's grip, but he held tight as he ordered Reese to drop his pack.

Movement in the brush to their left had Grayson pushing Laney to the side, drawing his weapon. Bursting through the brush, Jax rushed forward, intent on indicating the re-find.

She hated to do it, but for his own safety, she gave the emergency stop command using the hand signal and whispering, "Halt."

His stop was immediate. He dropped to the ground in a down position.

Tapping her chest twice, her silent recall signal, she motioned Jax to her.

Once Jax was by her side, the reality of the situation hit her hard. There was someone on the other side of the log, and he was armed.

Reese had dropped his pack and unholstered his weapon. Grayson drew them in a close circle, whispering, "Laney, mark our coordinates on your GPS, then take Jax back through the stand of trees. Move quickly and make noise as you go. When you reach the stream, take cover and call base for backup. Reese, you circle around the fallen tree as quietly as you can from the left. I'll take the right. Don't be seen. Try to get in a position where you can see the shooter—when Laney is out of earshot, he may make a run for it. Be ready."

Reese nodded.

Laney turned to go, but Grayson grabbed her arm and pulled her close. "Don't come back until I call you."

She nodded her understanding, but he didn't let her go. His gaze was dark, his ocean-blue eyes filled with concern.

He cupped her cheek, his fingers rough and a little cool. "Be careful, okay?"

She swallowed down words that she knew she shouldn't say, words about friendship, about connection, about wanting to know that this wouldn't be the last time she'd ever see him.

"You, too," she whispered to his back as he quietly headed for the downed tree.

She headed in the opposite direction, crashing through the underbrush.

"Jax, come!" she yelled, and the dog followed.

She reached the other side of the trees, took cover behind a giant oak and called for backup, providing the coordinates to base. Her voice shaking, she made sure the other dog teams understood they should stand down and stay away from the sector.

"Laney?" Kent's voice came over the radio.

"Go ahead, Kent."

"We have four officers stationed on the road in your vicinity—we're sending them in now. Stay where you are until they get to you."

They arrived quickly, slipping through the woods almost silently. Only Jax's soft huff of anxiety warned her before they appeared.

"Where's the perp?" a tall, dark-eyed man asked. She was sure she'd seen him before, had probably worked with him at some point.

"Follow me, and be as quiet as possible." Laney led the officers around the thickest part of the brush in an attempt to keep down the noise. They followed her one by one, in silence. She stopped, the fallen tree fifty feet in front of their location, roots snaking out four feet in every direction, ensnared with thick underbrush. Turning to them, she whispered, "The suspect is holed up behind that downed tree." She pointed. "Agent DeMarco went to the right, Officer Reese to the left. They intended to get a visual of the suspect and wait for backup."

"Okay. We've got it from here. I want you to take cover behind that stand of trees, then radio base that we are here and in position."

Laney nodded. Then the officer in charge turned to his guys. "Radio silence from this point on." Several of the officers turned their handheld radios off.

Laney crept to the stand of trees, finding a hiding place under a particularly thick bush. Then she called base, confirming the team's position. Motioning Jax to sit by her, she absently petted his head while she waited for something to happen. Anything.

Suddenly a voice broke the silence. Grayson's voice.

"This is the FBI. You're surrounded. Throw out your weapon and release the child."

"I'll kill the kid if you come any closer."

"Not before we kill you, so how about you make it easy on yourself? Send the boy out!" Grayson's last statement was met by a warning shot from the suspect.

It was then that Laney noticed the brush moving near the bottom of the fallen tree, where thick weeds and saplings were growing up around it. Could there be another way for the suspect to get out? If so, Grayson and the other officers were not in a position to see the suspect escape. Seconds later, a blond head popped out.

A child's tear-streaked face appeared as the boy pushed through the thick brush. Giving Jax the signal to stay, she grabbed her Leatherman out of her pack and opened it. She eased across the space that separated her from the tree and saw the boy's eyes widening with surprise as he spotted her. Holding a finger to her lips, she signaled him to stay quiet as he came out of the opening under the tree and stood. An adult's tanned hand was visible through the brush, grasping the boy's ankle. Laney readied herself, watching the brush move, the leaves rustle.

Was she the only one who noticed the movement?

Suddenly, the kidnapper's head and other hand pushed through the opening. That hand grasped a gun. He never released his hold in the boy's ankle as he snaked through the brush. The child stood still, blue eyes wide with fright, trained on her. Laney didn't intend to let the kidnapper make it out from under the tree. She took two steps closer and stomped with all her might on his hand.

He cursed, the gun dropping from his slack hand.

She kicked it away and grabbed the boy's arm, yanking him from the kidnapper.

"Run!" she screamed.

EIGHTEEN

Hoisting himself quickly to the top of the downed tree, Grayson could scarcely believe what he was seeing. Hadn't he told her to stay by the creek? To wait in safety until he called her? She hadn't, and she was about to be taken down by a guy who looked like he'd gladly drag the knife from her hand and use it to slit her throat.

Grayson scrambled over the tree and tackled the guy as he lunged for Laney and the boy.

They all went down in a heap, tangled in weeds and thorny brush.

The guy was big. Maybe six-foot-four, muscular.

And angry.

He pushed himself to his knees and threw a punch; Grayson dodged it, the man's knuckles barely grazing his jaw. Grayson managed to land a well-placed blow to the man's cheek. The guy fell backward, knocking into Laney as she scrambled to her feet, grabbing the boy under the arm to drag him from the fray.

She stumbled. Falling to her knees, she shoved the boy out of reach. The kidnapper's arm shot out and grabbed Laney's calf. She tried unsuccessfully to kick him off while Grayson punched the guy in the back.

The man cursed but didn't relinquish his hold on Laney. He yanked her toward him across the brush like a rag doll.

Grayson heard Laney gasp. Her chest hit the ground first, knocking the wind out of her.

Grayson landed a quick blow to the perp's head, and then another. Other than a faint grunt, there was no acknowledgment that the hits had any effect on the guy. Behind Grayson, the other officers were crashing through the brush to help.

The man relentlessly dragged Laney toward him, ignoring the kicks from her free leg.

Grabbing the guy in a choke hold, Grayson yanked him backward. Still he refused to release Laney.

Laney looked up, meeting Grayson's gaze over the perp's shoulders. He recognized the anger and determination he saw there. Without warning, she sliced her pocketknife across the guy's hand. With a howl, he let go of her leg.

She scrambled away and rushed to the boy, who stood watching wide-eyed by a tree. Grayson tightened his grip around the guy's neck. Reese nudged in beside Grayson, taking cuffs from his belt. He snapped them onto the suspect's wrists and pulled him to his feet.

"Hey! That crazy chick cut my hand! I need a medic!" the perp howled.

"You'll get one." *Eventually*, Grayson thought, but he didn't say it.

He was too busy striding to Laney's side, taking the knife from her hand. "Are you nuts?" he nearly shouted. "You could have gotten yourself killed!"

"What was I supposed to do?" she asked, touching the hair of the little boy who was clinging to her waist, his head buried against her abdomen. "Let the guy escape with Carson?"

"What you were supposed to do was stay away," he reminded her. "Until I told you differently."

"If she had," the boy said, shooting Grayson a dark look, "she couldn't have rescued me."

"I didn't rescue you. Jax did," Laney said. "Want to meet him?"

"Who's Jax?" Carson asked.

"I'll show you. Jax, come," Laney called, and the dog bounded out from the underbrush.

"He's so cool!" Carson dropped to his knees to pet Jax, his face suddenly animated. "When we saw the dog the first time, that guy made me hide under that tree with him so the dog wouldn't know where we went. He said I had to stay quiet or he'd kill me."

Grayson kneeled on the ground next to Carson. "So you did what he said, right?"

Nodding, Carson hugged Jax. "I was afraid of him. He was mean. He tried to shoot the dog, but I hit his arm so he would miss."

Laney went to her knees too, enveloping the boy and dog in a big bear hug. "Thank you for saving Jax."

"I knew Jax was good. We learned about search dogs in Boy Scouts. I knew he would bring me help, and he did."

"Yep, he did his job well. Now he gets his reward. Do you want to help me give it to him?" Laney asked.

"Sure, what is it?"

She pulled out two orange balls, squeaking them.

Jax turned toward the sound, ready to run.

"He gets playtime with his favorite toy for a job well done."

She chucked the ball as far as she could, and they both laughed as Jax rushed forward, jumping up and snatching it out of the air before it hit the ground.

Squeaking it in his mouth, the dog returned, dropping the ball at her feet as she launched the next one in the air.

"Grab that ball, Carson, and throw it as soon as he brings the other back—let's see who gets tired first, him or us!"

Grayson was betting on the two of them, since the ball of energy that was Jax showed no sign of stopping anytime soon.

Watching the woman who would likely never fail to surprise him, laughing and playing with the dog and the boy
in the midst of what should have been a very traumatic day
for all, Grayson realized Laney's affinity for dogs trans-
lated to children as well. Her fearless confidence and her
empathy for the helpless attracted both to her. And right
now, with this boy, she was managing to single-handedly
end his bad day on a good note.

Although there were many people who had worked together to find and rescue Carson, Laney and her hero dog
Jax would stay with the boy always. As he grew older and
recounted this story, Laney would always be in it. His own
fearless protector.

Funny. Grayson's story about the day would be the
same.

Empty of the million little details that had made the
rescue successful, and filled with hundreds of images of
a woman he knew he would never forget.

Noon, and Laney was exhausted.

She should probably get up from the porch rocker and
go inside, but she was too tired to move. Grayson and
Kent were a few feet away, talking to the two FBI agents
assigned to her protection detail for the next few days.
The sun had grown warmer, but dark clouds rolled in on
a humid breeze, threatening rain.

Tonight would mark forty-eight hours missing for Olivia.

Two days of tracking one clue after another, but never
seeming to get closer to the answers they needed to bring
Olivia home. Laney was frustrated, irritated, antsy to see
progress made on the case.

She had sensed some frustration in Grayson, as well. He
hadn't been happy that the kidnapper's interrogation had
been put on hold to treat his hand. Laney was sorry that

the interrogation would have to wait, but she couldn't say she completely regretted the bone-crushing stomp to his hand that had apparently broken two fingers. She didn't regret cutting him, either. He'd deserved it, and worse, as far as she was concerned. She only hoped that Grayson and Kent would be able to uncover some link between this kidnapping and the others.

One thing was certain. Today's kidnapper was not the same man who took Olivia.

Kent and Grayson came up the porch stairs, the two FBI agents right behind them. "Laney, if it's okay with you, we'd like to use your house to have the FBI agents work with Arden and me on reviewing some of the case files that were faxed over this afternoon…the more eyes the better," Kent said.

"Make yourselves at home," she responded, gesturing to the front door.

The three other men walked inside.

Grayson stayed put, his gaze on Laney.

"You don't really think I'm going to leave you out here alone, do you?" he asked.

"I was hoping."

"Tired of all the people in your house?" He reached for her hand, tugging her to her feet.

"Tired, period." She would have stepped away, but he pulled her closer, looked straight into her eyes.

"From the search?"

"From everything."

"Was it hard?" He traced a line from her ear to the corner of her jaw, his hand sliding down and resting on her nape. He kneaded the tense muscles there.

"Stopping the kidnapper?" she asked, her mind more on his touch than on his questions.

"Going back to search and rescue."

"It was as easy as taking my next breath," she admitted, and he smiled.

"I thought it would be."

He opened the door and let her walk inside ahead of him. They followed the sound of voices into the dining room.

Arden was there, Kent and the two FBI agents a few feet away, watching as she systematically stacked documents on the table.

Arden placed the last piece of paper in the pile and finally looked up.

"There. I've organized these records by date and placed the original records we received today via fax in front of the records Grayson downloaded from his system. This is how I propose we tackle the review." She was interrupted by Grayson's phone.

He glanced at his caller ID and frowned. "Excuse me, everyone. I need to take this call."

Laney watched him walk away and fought the urge to follow. It still bothered her that she was relying on him so completely, but not as much as it might have a couple of days ago. She realized now it was okay to accept help when needed. And deep down, she knew she would be all right when he was gone. Even though a small part of her would be sad to see him go, she would always be grateful for what he'd done. Not just protecting her, but helping her get back to the person she wanted to be.

She'd taken the first step in moving on. She'd brought herself and Jax out of retirement. Maybe it was time to take the next step and join another search and rescue team here in Maryland. When this was over, she'd have to thank Grayson for helping her remember that some things were worth fighting for.

"DeMarco," Grayson said, pressing the phone to his ear. If it had been anyone else, he wouldn't have taken the call, but it was Ethan, and Grayson would do anything for his friend.

"Gray, its Ethan. How are things going?"

"We might have something to go on. We stopped a kidnapping today. The perp will be brought in for questioning after he's released from the hospital."

"Do you have evidence that he's connected to the other kidnappings?"

"No."

"Could be coincidental."

"You know how rare stranger abductions are, Ethan."

"I do, but rare doesn't mean they don't happen," Ethan responded, a sharp edge to his voice. That surprised Grayson. In the years he'd known Ethan, he'd never known the man to be short-tempered or impatient.

"Either way, I have to look at every possibility."

"Right." Ethan laughed it off, any hint of impatience suddenly gone. "I actually didn't call to argue. I wanted to let you know it will likely be another day before I can get to the Maryland precinct—Judith's brother's in town, and she needs me to hang around and play host. If you can send me records, I can start to go through them for you."

"We've got a group of people comparing the hard copies with the electronic files I've been working with for months—I can have someone scan them in and send them to you if you think you'll have a chance to look at them."

"I'll make the time, Gray. Send them my way when you can."

"Thanks, Ethan, I'll talk to you soon." Grayson disconnected, less satisfied with the conversation than he usually was when he spoke to Ethan for some reason he couldn't quite define.

He shook off the unease, walking back into the dining room and taking a seat next to Laney.

"Great. You're here," Arden said. "Ready to work?" She handed him a stack of files. "This is our West Coast file."

Grayson started skimming the reports. Everything matched up until he reached the fifth page. There he found a name he hadn't seen before.

Ethan Conrad. Called in for consultation.

That's what the file said.

Why had Ethan failed to mention the consulting services to Grayson? Could there be a simple explanation? Maybe. But it didn't seem possible that he'd just forgotten. Even if he had, why was the information in one file and not the other? "Who has the original Boston files, months one and two?" he asked.

"I've got them," Kent said.

"Was any consulting company listed in the reports?"

"Not a company, but a man was mentioned. It was an FBI profiler, I think…here it is, Ethan Conrad."

Grayson skimmed the page, comparing this entry to the California entry.

Arden looked up at the mention of Ethan's name, catching Grayson's eye. "Ethan consulted on both those cases?"

"Yes. And that information was deleted from the doctored files."

"What about here in Maryland?"

Grayson grabbed the Maryland files, skimming them for Ethan's name, relieved when he didn't find it. Perhaps there was a legitimate reason for Ethan's involvement. "Nothing in Maryland."

But then, Grayson thought, there was no need to consult here in Maryland. Grayson had discussed the case at length with Ethan after taking over for the agents in Boston at Ethan's recommendation.

They talked almost daily, about everything. Ethan was a sounding board. A trusted advisor.

Could he also be a callous criminal?

Grayson's mind raced. He'd known Ethan for years, trusted him like family. There had to be another explanation.

Kent Andrews's phone rang.

He answered, his gaze focused on Grayson.

He was going to have to share his suspicions with Andrews. He had no choice. He had to run this lead down. If Ethan was innocent, he'd understand.

Andrews's phone conversation took less than a minute. When it was over, he smiled. "Good news, Grayson. We finally have a jailbird that's ready to sing."

"The suspect is talking?"

"Not just talking, singing like a jaybird! He said he was paid five grand to snatch a kid."

"Who paid him?" Grayson asked.

"A guy he met while incarcerated—David Rallings Jr."

"So our floater paid him to snatch a kid…"

"Yep, and deliver the kid to an access road near Camp Cone."

"Camp Cone is up there near Glenn Arm, isn't it?" Laney asked.

Grayson didn't answer.

He was too busy thinking, reaching a horrible and inevitable conclusion.

He'd spent a lot of summers at Camp Cone. He knew it well. The property was a little wild, a little rugged. He'd hunted squirrel there, hunted turkey, done all the things young boys liked to do.

And he'd done them all with Rick, because the property they spent their summers on, the little cabin where they used to stay, it belonged to Rick's parents. It belonged to Ethan.

He stood, pushing away from the table with so much force, his chair toppled over.

"Grayson?" Laney stood, touched his arm. "Are you okay?"

"It's pretty difficult to be okay when you've just realized that you've been betrayed by one of your most trusted friends."

"What do you mean?" Kent asked.

"Ethan Conrad owns property near Camp Cone."

Kent frowned, glancing at the report he still held. "The former FBI profiler? The same one who's listed as a consultant in these files?"

"He's not just listed there." Grayson set his paper down and pointed to the name. "He's listed here, too. But his name was taken out of the reports when they were tampered with. The hacker didn't want us to know that he was involved."

"Anyone else find his name in a report?" Kent asked.

"It's here," Laney said quietly.

He didn't have time to feel sorry for himself. Didn't have time to sit around moping. Ethan was one of the most intelligent men he knew, but even intelligent men made mistakes. "There's a cabin on Ethan's property, and an out-building used for hunting—either of those would be the perfect place to keep a bunch of kids," he said. "Arden, can you print me out a few topographical maps of the Glen Arm/Camp Cone area? And Kent, we'll need a search warrant to go on private property."

"I'll make some calls."

"How long do you think it will take?"

"A few hours? Maybe a day, tops—if we can convince them it's necessary."

"That's a long time if you're one of the kids he's kidnapped."

"I'll try to put a rush on it," Kent assured him.

"Good." Grayson glanced at the name, felt fury clogging his throat. "Because I suspect we found our leak, and the sooner we plug it, the happier I'll be."

NINETEEN

Later that evening, after poring through files with Arden and the FBI agents, Laney retreated to her room, claiming exhaustion.

Earlier, Kent had gone to the precinct to see if he could call in some favors and help expedite a warrant on Ethan's property. Grayson was trying a different tactic. He'd driven away over an hour ago, determined to convince a reluctant judge to issue a search warrant.

He'd left Laney behind.

Grayson had thought it would be safer.

It would have been. If she'd actually intended to stay there.

Low voices and murmurs of activity carried down the hall to her room. Rose was clanging in the kitchen while the others worked in the dining room. Laney carefully removed the screen from her bedroom window. When she was done, she retrieved her small search-and-rescue day pack from the floor beside her bed, shoved a pilfered topographical map of Camp Cone in it, then turned off the light, dropping the pack out the window to the ground. Grabbing her work cell phone from the charger on the dresser, she shoved it into her cargo pants pocket. The sun had just set below the horizon. The grass was damp from the late afternoon showers.

Laney's heart raced. Climbing onto the windowsill, she dropped to the grass. The night was quiet. So far, so good.

Laney knew Grayson would not approve of her intent to give her FBI and MPD babysitters the slip.

She also knew that the chance of Grayson getting a warrant on a respected, retired FBI agent based on the circumstantial evidence they'd collected was slim. She'd heard the agents talking about it being a pipe dream that a warrant would be provided in time to rescue the kids.

But Laney understood law enforcement and probable cause. If she and Jax happened to be hiking in the area and came upon something that could point to the children, Grayson would have all the probable cause he needed for an official search.

She was determined to make sure that happened.

Olivia's life was at stake.

Shrugging the pack onto her back, she whistled twice. She heard the soft pad of Jax's feet in the yard behind the house before he raced around the corner and sat attentively in front of her. "Good boy," she whispered. Patting her thigh twice, the signal for heel, she started off at a quick jog. Jax kept pace by her side. Laney ran through the trees, sticking close to the edges of the woods.

She needed to get to Aunt Rose's house and borrow her car.

Rose kept the keys to her 1974 Hornet hatchback on a peg in the garage. So as long as the keys were there, borrowing the car would be easy. Laney just hoped the Hornet would make the hour-long drive to Camp Cone. As far as she knew, Willow was the first person to drive the car in months, and she'd taken a five-minute drive to the grocery store.

Of course, it was a bit premature to worry about the car breaking down when she first needed to get into the garage. Laney was counting on finding the spare house key in its usual spot—buried in the topsoil under the decorated stone turtle in the back flower bed. Hurrying across the well-manicured back yard, she found the turtle right where she'd expected it to be. Beside her, Jax's ears perked up, standing at alert. His eyes watched the corner of the house. Someone was coming.

She jumped back into the shadows. There was no time to get the key. The soft sound of footsteps on the grass grew closer. "Laney?" As usual, Aunt Rose's whisper was scarcely a decibel under a yell.

"Shh!" Laney responded quickly. "Aunt Rose, what are you doing out here?" she hissed.

"Looking for you, of course." Reaching in her pocket, she pulled out a car key on a small fuzzy dice keychain. "I thought you might need this."

"How'd you know I was here—and why on earth are you carrying around a key to a car you can't legally drive?"

Aunt Rose planted her hands on her hips. "First of all, after the last break-in, I didn't want to leave the key where it could be so easily found—James is a classic, you know?" James, of course, referred to Rose's car. As Rose told the story, she'd purchased it the summer after her husband Peter died, because they'd watched James Bond together and he'd been fascinated by the aerial flip the car performed in the movie. Thankfully Rose had not yet attempted to duplicate that flip.

"Secondly," Rose continued, "I heard Gray and Kent talking to those agents, too. I'm not deaf, you know. As soon as I heard that they probably didn't have enough evidence to get a warrant, I knew exactly what you were going to do."

Lifting the stone turtle, Rose buried her fingers in the dirt below, coming up with the spare key to the garage. She absently wiped the dirt off on her pants. "Here you go."

"Does this mean you approve of the plan?" Laney asked, unlocking the garage and opening it.

Rose shook her head and sighed. "I'm not saying it's the smartest thing to do, mind you, but I know I won't be able to talk you out of it. You have too much of the Travis blood in you. Much more than your mama ever did, God rest her soul."

Taking the keys, Laney embraced her aunt. "Thanks, Aunt Rose."

"Honey, I know you've always worried that you might end up like your mother, but even as a girl, your mama was never strong. Not like you."

Shaking her head vehemently, Laney argued, "I'm not strong, I just try to do what needs to be done."

"Because you have an inner strength, girl. The grit and moxie your mom never had—that comes from here and here." She pointed to her head then her heart.

"Mom did her best."

"No doubt, but she married the wrong man."

"I know, and the sad thing is, I can see how it happened. My father could be a real charmer at times—you just never know what lies underneath."

"Laney, I think deep down you know that's not true. Some men are exactly as they seem. For instance, your grandfather—my brother—and my own husband."

"I'm sorry I never got a chance to meet Uncle Peter."

"Me, too, but I won't romanticize him—he was far from perfect. God knows none of us are perfect. But he tried to live God's plan for his life. That one simple act of faith made him perfect for me. Maybe you'll find the same to be true with Grayson."

"Aunt Rose, Grayson and I are just…" What were they? Working together? Friends? At times it seemed she'd known him forever. But really, did she know him at all?

"You can protest all you want, but you can't deny the attraction. But don't you think on it now. God's plan will unfold in its own time." She gave Laney a quick hug. "Give me two minutes before you start the car. I'll distract them with my new batch of grandma's whoopie pies."

"I love you, Aunt Rose."

"I know, and I love you, too."

Opening the car door, Laney motioned Jax inside. "Jax, place." Tail wagging, he hopped into the car.

Pausing at the entrance of the garage, Aunt Rose looked back over her shoulder. "Be careful, Laney. And leave the lights off until you get to the end of our drive. That's what I always do." Grinning, she was gone.

Grayson wasn't happy. He'd just left the judge's house— *without* a search warrant for Ethan's property. Despite the case Grayson had presented, the judge reasoned that Ethan appeared to have been a legitimate paid consultant on the cases, and that those records could have been doctored by anyone to cast the blame on Ethan. Furthermore, Camp Cone was a public park, backing up to several private properties, and since there was no evidence directly linking Ethan to any of the victims or suspects, the probable cause was not there. The judge sympathized but told Grayson he needed to make a stronger case for a warrant to be issued.

Grayson had a decision to make. He could follow the rules and keep searching for more substantial evidence to link Ethan to the crimes, or he could search the property himself, perhaps finding the kids, but knowing that anything he found couldn't be used in a court of law.

For the first time in his life, Grayson was thinking about breaking the law.

There had to be a way around this. There must be a way to rescue the kids and still bring Ethan to justice.

Ethan, who'd recommended Grayson for the case in the first place, then used his relationship with Grayson to monitor the progress the bureau was making and plan his next move. Grayson tamped down his fury. Rage wasn't going to help him figure things out. It wasn't going to make things easier. He needed to stay calm and cool-headed if he was going to beat Ethan at his own game.

And that must be what this was to his mentor—a money-making game that he had been playing and winning for far too long.

What was worse, logic dictated that this wasn't Ethan's first venture into organized crime. Grayson wondered when Ethan had turned. Had Rick's death sent him over the edge? Or worse, could he have had something to do with Rick's death? And Andrea's?

The thought turned his blood cold. Grayson had always wondered how Ethan had wrapped up the case of Rick's murder so quickly, so cleanly. The perpetrators had died trying to keep from being taken into custody, and there'd been no one to interrogate. There was no telling how deep Ethan's betrayal ran, but Grayson wanted the chance to ask him.

His cell phone vibrated. Kent's name and number scrolled across the dashboard display. He grabbed the phone, his hand shaking with the force of his anger. "De-Marco here."

"Laney's gone. She took one of the topo maps and Jax with her."

"What? How? There are four armed law enforcement officers at the house, and her Jeep is still in the impound lot!"

"She snuck out through her bedroom window while the FBI agents were in the kitchen with your sister and Rose. They were going through the case files, and she said she needed to lie down—"

"That should have been their first clue that she was up to something!" he snapped.

"Don't shoot the messenger, DeMarco," Andrews bit out. They were both tense, both disappointed with the judge's decision regarding the search warrant.

"The good news is," Grayson said, trying to calm himself down, "she couldn't have gone far without a vehicle."

"You're assuming she doesn't have one."

"Where would she get…" Grayson paused, realizing just how easy he and everyone else had made Laney's escape. "Rose."

"Rose admits to handing over the keys to her '74 Hornet hatchback, then distracting my officers with a plate full of whoopie pies and milk. Both of my guys are now complaining of stomach pains. I swear she's a menace with the baked goods."

Grayson's grip tightened on the steering wheel. "I'm not sure I care about your officers' stomach problems. How long ago did Laney leave?"

"She's been gone about ninety minutes."

"She's had more than enough time to get to the Camp Cone area, then. Has anyone heard from her since?"

"No. I tried to call her work cell. No answer."

Grayson banged the steering wheel, his frustration making him reckless. "What was she thinking?"

"According to Rose, Laney went to get us our probable cause."

That wasn't what Grayson wanted to hear. It wasn't what he wanted to think about. Laney and Jax searching Ethan's property couldn't lead to anything good.

"I just left the judge's house," he growled. "I can be at Ethan's property in less than fifteen minutes. I'm turning around now."

"I'm on my way with two patrol cars. We'll be there in thirty minutes, tops."

Disconnecting the call, Grayson tried Laney's work phone. Straight to voice mail.

He drove faster than he should have, faster than was prudent, speeding toward Camp Cone. Dozens of memories flashed through his head. All the times Ethan had seemed interested, concerned, helpful, he'd been playing Grayson for a fool.

He managed to make it to Camp Cone Road in thirteen minutes. It wove through an older, established neighborhood and dead-ended at the park entrance, where visitors could gain free public access during park hours. Grayson was betting that Laney would pick that as her entry point.

The access gate would have been locked at sunset, but Laney could easily have parked in the small lot and walked in. From there, she'd have to navigate about twenty acres of heavily wooded parkland to get to the boundary of Ethan's property.

Remembering how quickly and easily Laney and Jax had navigated the trees and brush during the morning's search, he was confident that she was well within Ethan's property line already. He was equally confident that he was ill-equipped to trail her through the woods.

No, he'd need to take the direct approach. He'd enter the property through Ethan's driveway and have a look around. At this point, he had no other choice.

The conditions were perfect. Temperature mild. A light, consistent breeze. Jax was definitely in scent. According to the compass and topographic map, they were less than fifty meters north of a man-made structure, possibly the hunting cabin that Grayson had mentioned. According to the map, it bordered the southern corner of Ethan Conrad's property. Laney decided that direction was as good as any to start. After all, if Ethan was hiding three children on the property, he'd need a secure place to keep them—a building away from the main house would be the best bet.

Laney didn't use a flashlight and did not turn on the lights on Jax's vest. Luckily, the night sky was clear, the almost full moon illuminating the woods. Jax's head popped up, and he stopped, nose to the wind. Over the light wind rustling through the trees, Laney thought she heard voices.

"Jax, come," she whispered. For a second Laney thought he wouldn't listen; she could see the reluctance as he looked at her, as if to say, "But the human is right there! Just a few more steps."

Laney touched her open hand to her chest, reinforcing her voice command with the hand recall command. This time Jax came.

"Heel," she said softly. They made their way slowly through the trees in the direction of the voices. The edge of the tree line was heavy with thick brush that made silence difficult. Jax moved through it easily, but Laney's clothing and hair caught on branches that snapped as she pulled away. Hidden within the tree line, she could just make out the outline of a very small, old outbuilding. Perhaps a one-room hunting cabin or large shed. If there were windows, she couldn't see them on the wall that faced her. No door, either, so she had to be looking at the back or side of the structure.

She crouched at the very edge of the trees, Jax beside her, his body tense with excitement. She scanned the clearing beyond the trees and spotted the source of the noise. Two men stood to the right of the structure, talking quietly. From her vantage point she could make out that the shorter of the two had a bald head. The other, bigger man was partially concealed by the building.

Headlights splashed light across a gravel drive choked with weeds. An uncomfortably familiar-looking dark panel van rolled toward the building, the driver guiding it into a position about a foot from the structure. He hopped out, then hurried to join the other men. Were they about to move the children? She would need to get closer if she hoped to learn anything. Both men disappeared around the corner of the structure.

She reached down and hoisted Jax into her arms, then took one slow, deliberate step at a time toward the edge of the tree line. She made it to a spot that was catercorner to the sliding panel door of the van. Setting Jax back on the grass, she gave him the hand motions for "down-stay" and crept toward the front of the structure.

She smelled cigarette smoke before she saw the third man. Seated in a folding camp chair, his back to her, he held the cigarette, its butt glowing orange in the darkness. Behind him, an open door revealed the black interior of the structure. Was someone in there?

"Hey!" the man called out, and she jumped, sure she'd been seen. "Hurry it up with those kids! We don't got all night to move them."

"They're not cooperating, so how about you get yourself in here and do something to help?" a muffled voice called from inside the structure. One of the three men she'd already seen? Or a fourth person?

"Do I gotta to do everything?" the man with the cigarette called back. He took a deep drag on the cigarette, tossed it onto the ground and crushed it under his foot. "You tell those brats I'm coming in. One more complaint from them and I'll set this whole place on fire with them in it."

"You don't do squat!" A man appeared in the doorway, and she recognized him immediately. The man who'd grabbed Olivia.

Silently pressing herself to the shadows of the building, she held her breath, praying that she wouldn't be seen.

"I do plenty. But if I got to help you load the brats, I'll help. Ship departs Baltimore at 6:00 a.m. We don't got a lot of time," the man said.

At that moment, the third man came out of the out-building, spouting a string of obscenities. He was bald, older than the other two, and smaller, but somehow more threatening.

"How about you two stop chatting and get back to work? In two hours, you can take your money and go your separate ways. For now, you'd better stick to the plan. Get in there and search the hold room for any evidence they may have left behind. We leave in ten. Either of you girls wants to slack off now, I can arrange for you not to leave at all."

The three entered the structure. The door slammed shut behind them.

Rushing to the tree line where Jax patiently waited, Laney pulled her cell phone out and powered it up. She had less than ten minutes to figure out how to stall the men. If they left, she'd have no way to follow them. She'd parked Aunt Rose's car a good twenty-minute trek back through the woods.

She could call 911 or she could call Grayson. She made the decision quickly, dialing the number and waiting as the phone rang twice.

"Laney! Where are you?" Grayson voice boomed through the phone.

"I'm at Ethan Conrad's property, and the kids are here."

"You've seen them?"

"No, but I saw Olivia's kidnapper and the van with the dented front end. The kidnappers are moving the kids to the Port of Baltimore. They'll be shipped out from there."

"When?"

"All I heard is that the ship leaves at six. I'm not sure what time they'll be loading the kids, but they're planning to leave here in ten minutes."

"I'm on my way. So is Andrews. I need you to get back to the woods and stay out of sight."

"Grayson, if I do that, the kids will be gone before you get here."

"And we'll have people at the Port of Baltimore waiting for them."

"The Port of Baltimore is huge. You'll never find them."

"Don't argue, Laney!" he growled. "You've given me the probable cause I need. Now step aside and let us handle things."

"I'll...stay safe," she said. "I've got to go. They'll be out with the kids any minute."

Laney disconnected and turned off the phone before shrugging out of her day pack.

Reaching into the front pocket, she pulled out a plastic Ziploc bag containing her NASAR-required first-aid kit. It included three extra-large safety pins. Fishing them out, she returned the rest of kit to her day pack. If she could wedge a safety pin or two firmly into a tire's valve stem, the air would be released slowly, possibly causing a flat tire before the men reached the port. She knew she had only minutes to make this work.

Ducking behind the front passenger tire, she quickly unscrewed the tire's valve cover. Then, using the tip of the safety pin to push down the valve core, she wedged in the pin to keep it from popping up. It held, but felt loose, so she shoved in the second pin. Better, but it would likely not hold when the tire began rotating at sixty-five miles an hour. Grabbing her last safety pin from her pocket, she opened it and forced it between the first two pins.

Solid. Holding her finger over the air valve, she could feel the slight but steady rush of air pushing out. The question was, if it held, how long would it take before the van was inoperable?

The door to the building was flung open. "I'll be at the van. Get those kids ready to move," someone called out.

Laney was out in plain sight with no choice but to run.

She darted away from the van, aiming for the tree line and Jax.

She didn't make it.

He was on her in an instant, tackling her to the ground so hard, every bit of air was knocked from her lungs.

He grabbed a fistful of her hair and yanked her head up so he could look at her face. "You!" he spat.

"What's going on?" The bald man stepped outside, two children beside him.

"Nothing I can't handle." The kidnapper pulled out a gun, pressed it to her head.

"Are you nuts? Put that thing away. We kill her here and there will be blood evidence everywhere. That happens and Conrad will put a mark on each of us. We'll be dead by sunrise."

The kidnapper cursed but hauled Laney to her feet. "I guess you've got a better plan?"

"Sure do. We sell her. Just like we're doing with the kids. We needed five live bodies. Now we've at least got four."

"Right. Fine. Whatever." The kidnapper shoved her toward the van with enough force to knock her off her feet.

She went down hard, her palms skidding along gravel, bits of dirt digging into her flesh.

A fast-approaching vehicle barreled down the access road, high beams blinding. Laney could only pray it was the cavalry.

TWENTY

Grayson assessed the situation as his car barreled toward the old hunting cabin, high beams on in an attempt to blind the suspects.

Two men were loading kids into a van.

Laney was on the ground. He could see her clearly, and for a moment, he thought the worst.

Then she popped up and tried to run toward the trees.

A man grabbed her around the waist and hauled her toward the van. Another man jumped into the driver's seat.

Hitting the brakes, Grayson flung open the driver's door, pulled his service revolver and trained it on the guy who was manhandling Laney. "FBI. Throw your weapons down and put your hands in the air."

A third man ran out of the building and fired a shot at Grayson.

Laney screamed. Out of the corner of his eye, Grayson saw a brown-and-white ball of fur in a bright orange vest running in. Jax took hold of the kidnapper's pants leg while he struggled to push Laney into the van.

"Do something about this mutt!"

The bald guy turned, taking aim at Jax.

"No!" Laney yelled. "Jax off. Away!"

Jax immediatcly let go, backing away, the bullet miss-

ing him by mere inches as Laney was shoved in the van.
The door closed behind her.

The man in the doorway of the building fired another
shot. Grayson aimed and pulled the trigger.

The man went down, and the van took off, leaving the
fallen kidnapper where he lay.

Grayson couldn't shoot at the van and risk a stray bullet hitting Laney or one of the children.

The perpetrators weren't as worried about that.

One of them leaned out the passenger side window and
fired another shot at Grayson as the van barreled past.
Grayson dove for cover, but the bullet dug into his shoulder, before he hit the ground. Pulling himself to his feet,
he called in his location and the direction the perps were
heading.

Blood oozed from the wound, but he didn't feel any
pain. Couldn't feel anything but rage and fear.

"Jax, come!" he called.

The dog rushed to his side, looking up at him.

Grayson scooped him into his arms and deposited him
on the passenger seat of his car.

His cell phone rang as he sped after the van. He took
the call.

"DeMarco. Go ahead."

"It's Kent. I've got dozens of men heading to Conrad's
place. Do you have Laney?"

"They've taken her and the kids to the Port of Baltimore," Grayson answered. "I'm headed there now."

"All right. I'll divert my guys there," Andrews acknowl-
edged. "Do you still need resources at Ethan's property?"

"Send a patrol car and an ambulance. We've got one
perp down." He didn't mention his own wound. It didn't
matter. All that mattered was closing in on the van and
getting Laney and the kids out of it safely.

"Will do."

"Can you also send someone out to Conrad's full-time residence? He's in Silver Spring." Grayson rattled off the address. It was as familiar as his own.

"Consider it done," Kent confirmed. "Do you have a visual on the van?"

"Not yet, but I'm moving fast."

"Where do you want us to meet you?"

"The Maryland Port Administration offices on Pratt Street. Someone's going to tell me which ships are leaving Baltimore at 6:00 a.m., and from which docks."

Grayson had been driving at a fast pace for about twenty minutes without seeing the van. That worried him. Had Ethan changed the plans? Had he caught wind of what was going on and decided to move the kids somewhere else? Taking Charles Street, Grayson exited to Pratt Street, where he would meet Andrews.

And there it was.

Abandoned on a side street, the panel van had one pancake-flat tire.

Pulling up behind it, he got out and touched the hood of the vehicle. Still warm.

He crouched near the tire. Safety pins had been jammed in the stem.

Laney. She'd put herself in jeopardy to sabotage the van. A smart move, too, since the Port of Baltimore was one of the largest ports in North America. There was no way the perps could parade around the docks with four hostages in the middle of the night and not draw attention to themselves. They would need another vehicle to get the kids and Laney to the loading dock undetected.

Another vehicle didn't just happen. They'd have to find one.

Which meant that they'd stash the kids and Laney somewhere close by.

He tried the van door and found it unlocked. Laney's

cell phone lay on the floor. He left it there and put in another call to Andrews.

He gave the location of the van, his communication quick and to the point.

They didn't have time to waste.

When he finished, he walked back to his vehicle. Jax, still in his bright orange vest, waited there, the equivalent of a homing beacon. "You want to work?" he asked the dog.

He was rewarded by an enthusiastic thump of the tail.

"Good. Me, too." He lifted the dog out of the vehicle, ignoring the stabbing pain in his shoulder as he set him on the ground, then issued the command as he'd seen Laney do. He pointed to the van. "Jax, place!"

Jax leapt inside and immediately seemed to pick up on Laney's scent, going right to her cell phone with a little whine, then pressing his nose in all the rear seats of the vehicle.

Finally, when it was apparent Laney was not in the van, Jax sat down beside her phone, looking sadly at Grayson.

"Where's Laney?" Grayson asked.

At the sound of her name, Jax cocked his head. His ears perked up.

"Laney?" he repeated. He knew Jax was an air scent dog, not a tracking dog. He could only hope Jax understood what Grayson was asking him to do.

Jax barked and stood, tail wagging, tongue lolling. Grabbing Laney's phone, Grayson put it up to Jax's nose. When he was done sniffing, Grayson dropped the phone in his pocket. "Jax, go find Laney!"

Grayson didn't have to tell him twice. Jax leapt from the van, put his nose to the ground, then to the wind, then back to the ground, and started across the street, heading straight toward a warehouse. Grayson could see the door had recent damage, as if someone had taken a crowbar and pried it open. Testing it, he found it unlocked. He drew his service revolver and stepped into the dark interior.

* * *

It was almost pitch black and a little cool in the storage room where Laney and the kids were waiting.

Laney pressed her ear to the door, trying to hear into the warehouse beyond their prison. She was pretty sure at least one of the bad guys was in the vicinity. The other had gone to find a new vehicle. He hadn't been happy when the tire went flat.

Laney had the bruise on her cheek to prove it.

She couldn't feel the pain of it. All she could feel was the panicked need to escape the room, to get the kids to safety, to make sure that Grayson was okay. She tried the door handle again. Locked. Still.

There had to be a way out. Had to be.

She turned back to the kids, felt something slap against her thigh, felt a moment of hope so pure and real that she nearly shouted with the excitement of it.

Her emergency penlight. She always carried it on searches. She yanked it from her cargo pocket and flashed it across the three huddled kids.

"Don't worry," she said. "I'm going to find a way out of this."

She hoped.

She shone the light on the floor and pointed it into the dark corners. Boxes lined the walls and took up most of the floor space. Trails of rat droppings and dust dotted the old tiles. There was only the one door, but maybe there was a vent she could shimmy through, some other way of escaping. She flashed the light onto the ceiling. Old 1970s panels threatened to fall out of the drop ceiling.

Perfect!

Laney knew that if she could get to the top of the wall and push up a tile, all that would separate her from whatever was next door would be more tiles. She thought about dropping straight into the warehouse, but she didn't know where the kidnappers were. Four lives depended on her escaping without notice—including her own. She could climb over the support beam and drop into the next room. Ideally find an unlocked door there and move into the warehouse, where she'd find a way to smuggle the kids out.

She turned the light back in the direction of the kids.

They looked terrified, their faces streaked with grime, tears and, in some cases, a few bruises. Olivia was hugging a girl who looked much smaller and younger than she was. Laney recognized her from the Amber alerts and news stories surrounding her abduction. Eight-year-old Marissa James. The dark haired, slim boy standing beside them was eleven-year-old Adam Presley.

"I need you guys to help me move some of those boxes to the corner," Laney whispered. "We need to stack them so I can climb up."

She flashed the light so they could all see the area.

The kids moved quickly and more quietly than Laney expected.

Fear was a powerful motivator.

It didn't take long to create a sturdy platform. "I'm going to climb through," she whispered. "Once I make it to the other side, I'll unlock the door."

"Why can't we all climb through?" Adam asked. "If you go and don't come back—"

"I'll come back."

"But if you don't," Olivia whispered, "we're stuck."

"I will either open this door and get you out or come back through the ceiling. Either way, I'm not leaving anyone behind." She meant it. And she hoped she could follow through.

If something happened, and she was killed...

It was a thought she couldn't dwell on. God was in control. He saw. He knew. She had to believe that He'd act.

Laney said a quick prayer as she hoisted herself to the top of the storage room wall. She removed the drop ceiling tile, carefully handing it down to Adam. Using her penlight, she peered over the wall into an office space. It was empty. Pocketing her light, she started to formulate the best plan for lowering herself down to the next room.

The telltale sound of clicking of paws moving rapidly across the concrete floor grabbed her attention.

Could it be?

Had Grayson and Jax somehow found the warehouse?

And where was the kidnapper with the gun?

Her question was answered when the guy lumbered into the office, closing and locking the door behind him, then quietly peering through the blinds of a window that opened into the warehouse.

Jax was out there. Laney knew it, and she thought Grayson was with him. She hoped he was. She'd overheard one of the kidnappers say he'd shot him. If he was in the warehouse, he'd survived, but he was also a sitting duck. There were windows in the interior office wall that looked out into the warehouse. If Jax and Grayson walked by where the kidnapper could see them… Her blood grew cold at the thought.

She scrambled back down into the storage room.

"New plan," she whispered to the kids. "The kidnapper is in the room next door. I'm heading into the warehouse. I'll open the door when I get to the other side. When I do, everyone needs to leave single file and quietly. Hug the wall to the right, hold hands and stay together."

Removing her boots so her drop to the floor would not be heard, she climbed through the open ceiling tile and sat on the top of the wall. It was a good eight-foot drop. She lowered herself until she was hanging by her hands, her socked feet dangling about three feet from the floor. Holding her breath, she prepared to let go.

* * *

Keeping to the edges of the open warehouse, Grayson followed Jax toward a row of offices. Jax looked up.

Grayson followed his gaze and saw a pair of legs dangling from an open panel in the ceiling.

Laney!

He rushed forward, touched her ankle.

She let out a bloodcurdling scream, and the silent warehouse suddenly turned to chaos. Kids screamed from the other side of a closed door. Distant footsteps pounded on old tile.

Grayson yanked hard enough to pull Laney down, catching her as she tumbled into his arms.

"Grayson!" she cried, throwing her arms around his neck. "I thought you were dead."

"Not yet, but we both might be if we don't get moving."

"The children!" She broke away and unlocked and opened a door.

Three kids emerged, all of them in various states of hysteria.

An office door opened. The kidnapper rushed toward them, gun in hand.

"Everyone down!" Grayson hollered.

Laney, the children and even Jax hit the floor, leaving the gunman an easy target. Grayson got off his shot first. The man went down. But there had been two men in the van earlier. Where was his accomplice?

Thundering footsteps were getting closer, and Jax growled, sensing danger before any of them could see it.

Grayson scooped up the smallest child in his left arm, wincing as she latched onto his wounded shoulder. There was cover of sorts near the edges of the warehouse, where the shadows were deepest and machinery crowded the floor.

"Come on!" he urged.

Laney grabbed the hands of the other two children and followed Grayson closely.

Somewhere in the distance, a door opened and closed. Feet tapped on concrete. Not one set of footsteps. Several. Grayson was maintaining radio silence, but he'd called the warehouse location in, and he knew the cavalry had arrived. He just had to keep the kids and Laney safe until Andrew's men could take Conrad's remaining thug down.

Hugging the shadows, he led them down a shelf-lined corridor, toward the emergency exit.

Behind them, a commotion ensued—shouts and gunshots as the remaining kidnapper met the cavalry.

Kicking open the emergency exit door, Grayson led them to the alley, where the flashing red and blue lights of the first responders were a welcoming sight.

They were met by police and paramedics, who took the children from their arms and ushered them to the safety of an ambulance.

Laney turned to Grayson, her eyes drawn to the blood dripping down his arm from his wounded shoulder.

"You're hurt!" She motioned to a paramedic, who grabbed her bag and headed toward them.

"It's not serious."

But Laney insisted he push up his sleeve and allow the paramedic to take a look.

"You've got a nasty gash," she said, removing a sterile pad and some gauze from her medical kit. "You need to have this properly cleaned and sutured. Looks like you've lost a considerable amount of blood, so I can't clear you to drive yourself."

Just then, Kent and two officers came out through the warehouse door, ushering the handcuffed kidnapper out into the alley and the waiting patrol car.

Kent jogged over to him as the paramedic finished field-dressing the wound and called for a gurney to be brought over. "Well, DeMarco, it looks like you're a little worse for wear."

"It's just a flesh wound. I'll be fine." Especially now that he knew Laney and the children were safe.

A second paramedic wheeled over a gurney. "It's time to go, sir."

Grayson sighed. "It looks like we're in for an ER visit," he said, reaching his hand out to Laney.

"We?"

"If you think I'm leaving you here on your own, you can forget it." He rubbed her palm with his thumb. "With your track record, that's much too risky—I need a vacation before I allow you to pull me into the next case."

Laney smiled, shaking her head. "I guess I had that coming." Her green eyes filled with laughter as she followed along for the ride.

TWENTY-ONE

Almost two weeks later, thanks in part to the computer forensic work Arden had performed on both the FBI networks and Ethan Conrad's personal computers and cell phone, there was enough physical and forensic evidence to get an indictment against Ethan and seventeen other accomplices. Charges spanned from murder to child trafficking. The previous night, Ethan, who had been stopped after crossing the border into Mexico and extradited to Maryland, had been charged with three counts of child abduction in Maryland, plus the thirteen others in Boston and California.

That was great news. Laney was glad Ethan was behind bars where he'd be unable to tear another family apart.

She smiled as she brushed her hair into a high ponytail and fingered the purple scar near her hairline. The staples had been removed, but it would be a while before the scar looked less raw and angry.

She didn't care.

All that mattered was that Olivia and the other kids were safe, and that there was hope of more children being recovered.

That Grayson...

She smiled again, because thinking about him always made her do that.

He'd recovered from his gunshot wound.

It might take a little while longer for him to get over Ethan's betrayal. Ethan's computer logs had revealed that he'd also been part of a money-laundering scheme his stepson had discovered. When Rick had confronted him, Ethan had killed him. Fearing that Rick had revealed information to Grayson, Ethan made an attempt on Grayson's life, too. His bullet had missed its mark and killed Andrea instead. Pinning the murders on two high-level gang members, he closed up the case while Grayson mourned his fiancée and friend, then continued, without missing a step, with his mentorship of Grayson.

It was a sad story that had come out in bits and pieces of forensic information—bank account records, phone records, the testimonies of some of Ethan's coconspirators.

Since the children had been recovered, there had been a whirlwind of activity—interviews with the press, law enforcement, judges and a prosecutor. Between that and work, Laney barely had time to think, but when she did, she found herself thinking about Grayson. Obviously he'd spent some time thinking about her, too. He called or visited almost every day. He'd even made it to the ceremony that morning.

Laney glanced at Jax, smiling at the little medal attached to his collar. The FBI had honored Jax, Arden and Laney for their part in recovering the children.

"But you're the only one who got a medal, Jax," Laney said, walking out onto the porch and taking a seat on the swing. Jax padded along beside her and found a comfortable spot in the sunlight. They'd trained hard the day before, and they were both tired. It was worth it, though. Being out of retirement made Laney feel more alive than she'd felt in years.

A car drove toward the house, and Laney recognized it immediately. Grayson had said he'd stop by when he finished work for the day.

One thing she was learning about him—he always kept his word.

Jax stood as the car parked, excited to see his new friend.

Grayson jumped out, his black hair gleaming in the sunlight, his face soft with his feelings for her.

He walked up the steps and took both her hands in his. "I've been waiting to do this all day," he said, pressing a sweet kiss to her lips.

She would have begged for more, but Jax nosed in between them, looking up with dark eyes and a silly grin.

"He looks great in his medal," Grayson said with a grin.

"Yes." She laughed. "He's been strutting around shamelessly since they put it on him."

"You, on the other hand," he said, "don't need a medal to look great. You're beautiful in fuzzy dog sweaters and weird leggings, with staples in your head and bruises on your face. You're beautiful out in the field with sunlight dappling your hair. And you're beautiful here, with your hair up and your face scrubbed clean."

"Grayson, I…"

"Don't make me stop, Laney. I might chicken out. There's something I want to tell you. I need to tell you. When I lost Andrea, I decided that was God's way of showing me that my plans for a family had to take second place to my career. For the past ten years, I've dedicated myself to this purpose God had for me." He touched her cheek, his fingers trailing down to her collar bone and resting there. "But something happened two weeks ago. It took a punch in the jaw from a pretty girl to bring me to my senses."

Laney laughed. "Yeah, sorry about that, but in my defense, I was concussed."

He smiled. "I had decided that because Andrea was taken from me, I wasn't meant to have a wife and family— to make promises to a woman that I might not be able to keep. I convinced myself it was God's plan for me to focus solely on my career, but the truth is, I was protecting myself from the possibility of finding someone and possibly losing them. I didn't want to hurt again the way I'd hurt when I lost Andrea. Her death left a hole in my heart."

"I'm so sorry, Grayson."

"I don't want you to be. I want you to know that you woke me up to the possibility that God might intend more for me. Everything happens according to plan, Laney, and meeting you, working together on this case, was all part of His plan.

"I can't promise you happily-ever-after, because the future isn't written in stone. But what I can promise you, Laney Kensington, is that if you take a chance on me, I will put your needs before my own, and I will protect you, and cherish you for the wondrously special and unique person that you are, for as long as I live."

Looking into his ocean-blue eyes, she saw the sincerity in them. His faith and strength of character were a constant, steadfast testament to who Grayson DeMarco was. And she knew that she believed him and trusted him with all her heart. Something that she never thought possible. She felt a tear fall before she realized she was crying.

He gently whisked the tear away with the pad of his thumb. "Why are you crying? Have I said something, done something…"

She shook her head and smiled. "I've never believed in happily-ever-after, Grayson, and I wouldn't believe anyone who offered it to me. But then again, I never used to believe in tears of joy, either, but you just wiped one off my cheek."

He kissed her then, gently, pulling her into his arms, then resting his chin on her hair. "Who knows, Laney? Maybe one day we'll both believe that happily-ever-after really is possible."

"Truthfully," she answered, "I think I already do."

* * * * *

Dear Reader,

I hope you enjoyed Laney and Grayson's story, *Into Thin Air*. This story is near to my heart for a couple of reasons. First and foremost, it is a story of faith and finding God's purpose in our lives. Laney has fallen into the trap that many of us stumble into—she has learned to rely on herself rather than God and closed herself to the possibility that God really did have a plan for her.

Second, this story speaks of the importance of trained and dedicated local, state and federal law enforcement officers and search and rescue personnel in times of crisis. Like many public servants, Grayson has found his purpose—to help bring justice and closure to families during their darkest hour. God's purpose for public servants is an honorable one that often requires sacrifice. This story not only delves into the sacrifices made by selfless, paid professionals but also highlights the important role that volunteer search and rescue teams and their dogs have in the quest to bring home the lost and missing.

Most of us will never have to deal with circumstances like those presented in this story, but my hope for you is that you will never forget God is faithful, His love is real, and His purpose for you will prevail, even in your own darkest hours.

Blessings,
Mary Ellen Porter

SECURITY BREACH
Capitol K-9 Unit • by Margaret Daley
A White House trespasser is on the loose, and tour director Selena Barrow teams up with Capitol K-9 Unit member Nicholas Cole and his trusted dog, Max, to track down the intruder...before his destructive plans are brought to fruition.

EXIT STRATEGY
Mission: Rescue • by Shirlee McCoy
Widow Lark Porter's set on finding her late husband's murderers—but she's quickly taken captive. Former army ranger Cyrus Mitchell will risk everything to rescue Lark...and bring her captors to justice.

BACKFIRE
Mountain Cove • by Elizabeth Goddard
Since testifying against a gang leader, Tracy Murray's been hiding as an Alaskan search and rescuer. When the crime boss's henchmen find her, Tracy turns to firefighter David Warren—who'll stop at nothing to keep her safe.

PAYBACK
Echo Mountain • by Hope White
Nia Sharpe's world is turned upside down when her estranged brother suddenly visits—with a dangerous drug cartel tailing him. Though her military veteran boss, Aiden McBride, acts as her protector, it also means he has become the criminals' next target.

PERMANENT VACANCY • by Katy Lee
Television host Colm McCrae doesn't know whether "accidents" keep occurring on set of Gretchen Bauer's B&B restoration because his boss is desperate to boost ratings—or because someone is out for revenge against the beautiful woman.

COVERT JUSTICE • by Lynn Huggins Blackburn
FBI agent Heidi Zimmerman has had enough of an infamous crime family's deadly schemes—it's time for her to go undercover. She knows two things—they're after Blake Harrison, and Heidi may be his only hope for survival.

Nicholas Cole hurried toward the White House special in-
house security chief's office in the West Wing, gripping the
leash for his K-9 partner, Max. General Margaret Meyer
stood behind her oak desk, a fierce expression on her face.

The general moved from behind her desk. "This office
has been searched."

He came to attention in front of his boss, having a hard
time shaking his military training as a navy SEAL. "Anything missing?"

"No, but someone had searched through the Jeffries
file, and it would be easy to take pictures of the papers
and evidence the team has uncovered so far."

"What do you want me to do, ma'am?" Nicholas knew
the murder of Michael Jeffries, son of the prominent
congressman Harland Jeffries, was important to the
general as well as his unit captain, Gavin McCord.

"I want to know who was in my office. It could be
the break we've needed on this case. With the Easter Egg
Roll today, the White House has been crawling with visitors since early this morning, so it won't be easy." She

shook her head. "Especially with the Oval Office and the Situation Room here in the West Wing being used for the festivities. If you discover anything, find me right away."

"Yes, ma'am." Nicholas exited the West Wing by the West Colonnade and cut across the Rose Garden toward where the Easter Egg Roll was taking place.

He scanned the people gathered. His survey came to rest upon Selena Barrow, the White House tour director, who was responsible for planning this event. Even from a distance, Selena commanded a person's attention. She was tall and slender with long, wavy brown hair and the bluest eyes, but what drew him to Selena was her air of integrity and compassion.

Selena would have an updated list of the people who were invited to the party. It might save him a trip to the front gate if he asked her for it. And it would give him a reason to talk to her.

Don't miss
SECURITY BREACH by Margaret Daley,
available June 2015 wherever
Love Inspired® Suspense books and ebooks are sold.

*Can a widow and widower ever leave their grief in the
past and forge a new future—and a family—together?*

Read on for a sneak preview of
THE AMISH WIDOW'S SECRET.

"Wait, before you go. I have an important question to ask
you."

Sarah nodded her head and sat back down.

"I stayed up until late last night, thinking about your
situation and mine. I prayed, and *Gott* kept pushing this
thought at me." He took a deep breath. "I wonder, would
you consider becoming my *frau*?"

Sarah held up her hand, as if to stop his words. "I…"

"Before you speak, let me explain." Mose took another
deep breath. "I know you still love Joseph, just as I still
love my Greta. But I have *kinder* who need a mother to
guide and love them. Now that Joseph's gone and the
farm's being sold, you need a place to call home, people
who care about you, a family. We can join forces and help
each other." He saw a panicked expression forming in her
eyes. "It would only be a marriage of convenience. The
girls need a loving mother and you've already proven you
can be that. What do you say, Sarah Nolt? Will you be
my wife?"

Sarah sat silent, her face turned away. She looked into
Mose's eyes. "You'd do this for me? But…you don't
know me."

"I'd do this for us," Mose corrected, and smiled.

The tips of Sarah's fingers nervously pleated and unpleated a scrap of her skirt. "But we hardly know each other. What would people think? They will say I took advantage of your good nature."

Mose smiled. "So, let them talk. They'd be wrong and we'd know it. I want this marriage for both of us, for the *kinder*. We can't let others decide what is best for our lives. I believe this marriage is *Gott*'s plan for us."

Sarah's face cleared and she seemed to come to a decision. She smoothed out the fabric of her skirt and tidied her hair, then finally took Mose's outstretched hand with a smile. "You're right. This is our life. I accept your proposal, Mose Fisher. I will be your *frau* and your *kinder*'s mother."

Don't miss
THE AMISH WIDOW'S SECRET
by Cheryl Williford,
available June 2015 wherever
Love Inspired® books and ebooks are sold.